THE DRACULA JOURNALS

Dark Decades

Books by Thom Reese

The Infusion of Archie Lambert
The Empty
A Savage Distance
The Demon Baqash
Chasing Kelvin
Dead Man's Fire
13 Bodies
The Crimson Soul of Nathan Greene

COMING SOON

The Dracula Journals Book 2

THE DRACULA JOURNALS

Dark Decades

Thom Reese

SPEAKING VOLUMES, LLC
NAPLES, FLORIDA
2016

THE DRACULA JOURNALS: Dark Decades

ISBN 978-1-62815-541-9

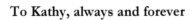

To Kathy, always and forever

ACKNOWLEDGEMENTS

However solitary the book writing process, there are always many people that help or influence the final finished manuscript. In this instance, I would be remiss if I didn't mention Bram Stoker first and foremost. His novel, Dracula, was not only the inspiration for this work, but is arguably the foundational vampire novel of all time. Every vampire novel since Dracula's publication in 1897 is derived in some way from the concepts of Stoker's masterpiece. And personally, it goes beyond this current volume. Dracula has always been one of my favorite novels. I particularly loved the epistolary style utilized by Stoker in which the novel is told through a series of journal entries and correspondences. This is what inspired my use of journal entries in my first published novel, The Demon Baqash. And so here I come, in some ways, full circle. I have written a sequel to the novel that inspired a major element of my first novel.

On a more personal level, I'd like to thank my wife Kathy, who always gives me solid feedback and direction. As well, my loyal friend and reader Jeff Granstrom helps me to dig deeper and find something better than I might have otherwise. His critique of earlier drafts had a huge impact on the final result. My daughters Trista, Amy, and Brittany give me joy and inspiration during the long hours pounding out a manuscript. That said, thank you Trista and Amy for your feedback on this particular project. Special thanks to Kurt and Erica Mueller from Speaking Volumes for your support and encouragement. I can't tell you how much I appreciate your efforts on my behalf. As well, I'd like to thank Amy Densham, Kym Low, and Travis Szynski for their ongoing support. And I would be remiss if I didn't acknowledge Anne Rice, Brian Lumley, and George R. R. Martin for writing vampire fiction that has inspired me.

The following is a collection of letters, journal entries, newspaper clippings, and other writings found in the home of Peter Van Helsing in August 2015. They have been organized in such a way as to allow the reader to best follow the sequence of events as they transpired. All entries unrelated to the topic at hand have been eliminated in order that these testimonies may stand on their own merit without distraction or confusion.

Letter from Hans Van Helsing to Larz Van Helsing
June 05, 1929

Dearest Larz,

I have seen them again. These things. These three women. The very ones that come out of the darkest of nights. The ones that call to me as with their minds. The ones that demand that I perform the most damnable acts. Oh my dear Larz, I am more and more convinced these are no mortal women. No creatures born of heaven or of this earth. More, they are as the animal. Howling into the night, clawing and loping and, I fear, devouring the innocent. Their skin, it gleams as the purest porcelain. Their teeth, they may well belong to the wolf. I know that they plague me because of Abraham's accursed chest. I know what it is they desire me to do. And, dear God, I fear that I may fall sway to their so wicked desires.

And so, I have determined to do a horrible thing. A thing that may forever damn my soul. I have not the strength of will, nor do I possess the character to destroy the thing. And even if I did, I sincerely doubt these midnight fiends would allow me to accomplish the deed.

But perhaps, just perhaps, if I were to remove the chest from their influence, if I were to bring it across the great sea and deposit it with our American cousins. Maybe the demon's sway would diminish. Perhaps I could finally live in some small peace. But my fear is this, that in doing so I may curse our relations. I can only pray that great distance will be our savior, that what the will of man cannot accomplish, the span of an ocean may achieve.

Pray for me, brother Larz. For I am feeble and despicable. May God forgive my weakness and protect our dear relative, for the boy cannot fathom the danger before him.

Your brother,

Hans

From the journal of Charles Van Helsing
October 16, 1929

This is a personal journal. I don't know if anyone will ever see these pages, but on the off chance that you, the reader, are not me, I guess I should probably start with some recent personal history. Maybe give you some sense of context before I address the troublesome and frightening writings that came to me from Europe and inspired me to keep this log.

My name is Charles Van Helsing. Charlie to friends and family. If you call me Charles I'll assume you either hate me or are a complete stranger.

Don't call me Charles.

Until a few months ago I was a student at Yale, attending on a scholarship and studying medical science. I know that sounds lofty but don't be too impressed. The fellas in my dorm certainly weren't. I was the first of the American branch of my family to attend a university. I did this entirely on scholastic merit as my family, though business owners, struggle financially and don't have the money for such an expensive education.

I loved the academic life. The lectures, the endless books, the research. I've always loved learning and though each member of my immediate family is an intelligent person, their gifts lie in areas outside of the classroom. To be honest, I've always been the oddball in my home, the one with my head filled with some equation instead of stuck under the hood of an automobile, the one reading Hemmingway while my brother reads Weird Tales magazine. But, I found my place at Yale.

That is, until my mother contracted pneumonia during my junior year. And though she survived the illness, it left her weak and unable to continue in her role as bookkeeper for the family business. I was horrified when I saw her for the first time after the illness. She smiled and patted my face, trying to comfort me. I saw hints of her spunk and humor, but her eyes were so sunken, her cheeks so hollow. It seemed she was so thin that her housedress nearly swallowed her.

I'll admit it. I was angry when Pop asked me to leave school to take Mom's place as bookkeeper. This was my future. My accomplishment. What right did he have to pull me away? But with him it always comes back to family. I can't argue with him about that commitment, but it didn't make it any easier.

My father, Vincent Van Helsing, owns a small chain of laundromats. And until recently, laundry was big business in the large industrial city of Chicago. But electric washing machines are now the rage in the more well-to-do homes and, on the other side of the nickel, the economy's sliding.

These changes would have ruined our family except for the existence of the eighteenth amendment. The Volstead Act. Prohibition. The ban on the sale and consumption of alcohol. Pop's involvement in bootlegging was spurred by a visit from his cousin Hans. (My brother and I call him Uncle Hans because he's in my father's generation, but he's really a second cousin. Or third. I can never keep that straight.) He's from the old country, Amsterdam, and is married to a German woman whose brother distributes liquor for a brewery.

Hans sat in our kitchen and said to Pop in his thick Dutch accent, "My friend, my cousin. We could work together, you and I. We can ship European liquor to you without detection from the authorities. The real product. Not that swill distilled in bathtubs or the watered down liquor sold by corrupt scoundrels. No, friend cousin. This would be pure."

Pop was hesitant at first. But Hans pressed on, talking about the huge profits of American bootleggers. Pop couldn't deny it. Everyone knew the story. Capone alone is said to make sixty million a year. Sixty million! Some say the number's closer to one hundred million. And here sat Uncle Hans saying, "Why shouldn't you get your share?" Pop had a hard time denying the logic.

As for me, mostly I keep the books. But those books include profits from my father's recently acquired shadow business. And sometimes my brother and I accompany Pop on midnight runs to either receive or deliver liquor.

Had I mentioned that I'm no longer at Yale?

My brother, Johnny, five years younger than me at seventeen, is much more excited about bootlegging than am I. To me it's a regrettable necessity, to him its glamor and excitement. During my three year absence he grew from an awkward acne-pocked kid to a slick young man, suave and confident, but idolizing people like Al Capone and Bugs Moran. Where just a few years ago he wanted to be a swashbuckler like Douglas Fairbanks, now he dresses like a gangster with his fedora, slick pinstriped suit, and high polished shoes. He talks like them too, imitating their slang and their tough guy attitude. He flirts with girls my age or even older and flashes money as if there's an endless supply.

Me, I have no use for flash. At five foot six, I'm not a big man. I carry a bit of a paunch, not much. I'm just a little beefy. Babe Ruth is a little beefy. Everyone likes him just fine. People either mistake me for shy or the strong silent kind. But really, it's that I just don't have much in common with most of the local fellas. I could care less about the latest prize fight or what hooch has the fiercest kick. I like women as much as any man but feel no need to brag about conquests or to hoot like an Amazon monkey at passing girls on the street. (This is never successful. Why do so many men persist in it?)

By and large I keep out of the main flow of the liquor business. Though Johnny's only seventeen, Pop confides in him much more so than he does me. Johnny's Pop's right hand man.

I could sulk about Johnny's close relationship with Pop and about being the fella on the outside, but if I'm honest with myself, I wouldn't want more involvement.

And besides, I have other interests.

One in particular concerns the writings I mentioned earlier.

They were in an old chest that Hans brought with him on a recent visit. He said that the chest had been taking up space for years and that the materials inside had belonged to my great uncle Dr. Abraham Van Helsing, as he put it, a scholarly man such as myself. And then he placed a palm on my shoulder, and with a barely perceptible tremor to his voice said, "Please take this from me. And if you are as smart as I think you to be, you will hide it away where it will never be seen." He turned away then and hurried from the room. In that moment I was too confused to fully comprehend what had just happened. It dawned on me much later that he was clearly fearful of the thing.

But, Hans is a dramatic sort and so I took his warning as one of his exaggerations. In truth, I was uninterested in the chest or its contents. It was probably just a bunch of old notes or maybe financial documents and other useless and uninteresting pages. The contents could be written in Dutch for all I knew. So, I lugged the heavy trunk off to my little corner bedroom and ignored it.

But finally curiosity got the best of me. Hans was dramatic, yes. But not normally fearful. And Mom kept asking about the chest. What had Hans said, had I opened it? Soon I began to wonder what could possibly be in there that would cause Hans such terror? And then, the next logical extension of this question, what could possibly be in there to cause such dread as to make him cart the thing across an ocean in order to be rid of it?

Well, I am if nothing else curious by nature. And once this thought was lodged in my brain it was only a matter of hours before I was kneeling before the thing determined to uncover the mystery.

The chest is made of dark wood, worn and bruised, cracked in three places, and was sealed with a padlock. I pounded the lock free with a hammer and then paused, staring at the ominous thing for perhaps a minute before reaching forward to lift the lid.

The aged container opened with a groaning creak and the contents offered a musty smell that sent me into a sneezing fit. At first I suspected that some of the papers might have been moldy because there were dark splotches on them. I've since reevaluated this conclusion, believing the stains instead to be blood.

Curious?

So was I.

Now, my great uncle Abraham Van Helsing is rather infamous. He's a featured character in Bram Stoker's popular vampire novel, Dracula. Yes, my relation was this same man. I've read the book. Of course I have. Our family name is all throughout the pages. But until recently I believed it to be fiction. Pop claims to know next to nothing about Abraham and scoffs at any connection to "a fictional character in a silly fairytale."

I used to believe Pop. But not since opening that chest.

You see, the chest contains the actual documents Stoker used to compile his Dracula manuscript. The writings of Jonathan Harker, of his wife Mina, of Dr. John Seward, of Lucy Westenra, and of course of my ancestor Abraham Van Helsing. Most of these writings had been copied over on the typewriter by Mina Harker and organized in chronological order so that a reader could gain a full understanding of the events surrounding the being known as Dracula.

To say that I was shocked by this discovery would be like referring to the Great War as a back alley squabble.

I can't describe the overwhelming sense of evil I felt when I first opened that box. Even before I'd discover the nature of the contents. It was as if a corrupt breeze whisked over me, tickling my arms, causing goosebumps to rise across my flesh. These were only old writings. Just timeworn pages. But my sudden fear nearly caused me to flee the room. I even considered burning the terrible things, whatever they were.

It took several minutes for curiosity to displace irrational fear. But once I'd regained my composure, I found that, if anything, I was now more curious than ever.

At first I could hardly believe what it was that I held. These were the actual journals and letters that comprised the book.

And so much more.

Many of the documents were very old, obviously dating to well before the birth of Uncle Abraham. These most ancient pages were written in another language, probably something Slavic. There were dozens upon dozens, all relating in some way to Dracula. I've spent weeks sifting through these and continue to find more and more remarkable discoveries.

Example: I found a letter from Abraham to his fellow vampire hunter Jonathan Harker. It'd been written near the end of my great uncle's life and gave detailed instructions on what to do with Dracula's remains which Abraham kept in an urn. Apparently he'd tried to disperse the ashes to the winds, but they were somehow bound together by some supernatural force and refused to scatter.

I'm not an expert on the supernatural. In fact, until opening this chest, I had no interest in, or belief in it at all. But what kind of strange magic could allow this dead creature to retain the will to collect his mortal ingredients? And why? To one day reassemble and rise again? Was that possible?

Apparently. For in another letter, Abraham urged Harker to take steps to ensure that Dracula never be reborn.

I was astounded.

Not only was I expected to believe that Dracula was a real historical figure, but that he could one day live again.

The implications fought against my rational mind and I continuously struggled to refute the evidence before me. For all of these years, I'd blindly assumed the vampire tale to be false, that the book had been a fiction, just a novel, the product of an imaginative mind.

But I'd been wrong. I don't know how Stoker came to be involved. Maybe he was a friend of my great uncle. Maybe he came across this very same chest in some other way. But the book had been written in the epistolary style, which means it was written as a series of correspondences and journal entries. I now had these very documents in my possession.

These and so many more.

I wasn't fully convinced. My mind is too pragmatic for that. But I was very curious. Driven even. If nothing else, the study of these documents gave me something to examine, some mystery to solve, something to occupy that area of my brain not utilized since Yale. Each evening I would lock myself away in my little shoebox of a room and study the seemingly endless supply of pages. Often skipping meals and ignoring family members.

This went on for weeks until one day I came across a set of neatly handwritten pages that changed everything.

Reading the heading, I came to realize the truth about one particular tome within the collection, a small leather book written in another language. Now my skin went cold as I realized what it was that I'd held. For these newer pages, written in my great uncle's hand, held the epitaph: "The Journal of Vlad Dracula as translated by Abraham Van Helsing."

That ancient journal which I had held, the one I had set aside because I couldn't read the language, it was the original writing. The one written by the vampire himself. I had in my possession the very journal of Dracula.

From the journal of Vlad Dracula
circa 1463 or 1464

I begin this memoir, not out of duty, or of some sense that there is any lasting value in my words but out of simple boredom. I am a prisoner and have far too much time to ponder my many victories and defeats. Damnable Mehmet and his overwhelming forces that he should have captured me. True, I was a fool, too overconfident, reckless, full of my own bluster. The fault is mine. Still, Damn

Mehmet and his forces. I am the rightful ruler of Wallachia and should be in my fair country with my beloved people. I should be guiding my generals in devising the overthrow of the wretched Ottomans. But here I sit, confined, unable to utilize my many gifts for any true purpose.

Oh, I realize I should not complain in excess. As prisons go it is not bad. This is not a dungeon but an estate. I am allowed access to the grounds, quite a bit of freedom and mobility just so long as I remain within the confines of the property. In fact, I have even met a woman with whom I am quite taken. Her name is Ilona. She is not a heathen such as the Ottomans, but a Christian such as I. But that, I suppose, should be told later.

Allow me to begin, as they say, at the beginning.

I am Vlad III Dracula son of Vlad II Dracul.

When I was a boy my father would often ruffle my hair and say, "Son of the dragon! You are as impetuous as your name sake." For Dracul means "Dragon" and Dracula means "Dragon's son." And yes, I was a rambunctious child.

In those days I was a happy lad, rowdy to be sure, and relatively carefree. It was a happy childhood, those few short years, filled with mock swordplay and raucous mischief. And in many ways seems as if it was a time that had never truly been. This sounds melancholy, I suppose, but I am a prisoner after all. I should be allowed a dark mood, I would think.

Everything changed when my younger brother, Radu, and I were accompanying my father on a diplomatic summit. I was eleven years of age. Radu was seven. He was just a little one, soft and fresh as an un-ripened peach. My father was then ruler of Wallachia and was therefore constantly on one mission or another, either tending to peace or war, whichever was the flavor of the day. He was a sworn member of the Order of the Dragon, a fellowship of knights tasked to defend Christendom against the Ottoman heretics and so held a dual responsibility both to the order and to his homeland. It is through this order that he received the surname Dracul.

The day was pleasant with a brisk breeze, bright sun, fresh horses, and plenty of food and water for the journey. The Danube glistened in the morning sun, the surface rippling just enough to disrupt the mirror-like surface. Birds sailed above, coasting on the gentle winds. Still my father was in a foul mood. Rarely did he respond to my playful jeers and taunts, and seldom did he meet the eyes of Radu, who was such a soft child and overly sensitive.

I though, wanted nothing of this somber tone and so took to wrestling with my younger sibling as we rode in the back of the carriage, tickling him and slapping his round little cheeks. "Pretty boy!" I giggled. "Such a pretty boy." Little did I know that as an adult he would be known as Radu the Handsome. Perhaps, in some way I contributed to this title, though I doubt it. To me he was never so much handsome as he was pretty. And weak. We must not forget weak.

"Quit it!" cried little Radu. "Father! Tell him to quit it!"

My father did more than to tell me to cease, he slapped me with the back of his hand sending me sprawling across the carriage seat. I could see that immediately he regretted this overreaction, for his deep set eyes softened and I saw the corner of his substantial lip twitch, but he was a proud man and stern. He would not admit to error or apologize to a child. I glared at him then, my eyes filled with disdain.

"Tend to your mouth, little dragon," he said. "There is blood on your lips." Blood on my lips. Small wonder where that came from. There was likely some of the same on his knuckles.

Upon arrival we were escorted into the inner chambers of Sultan Murad II. My first impression was of how very different the sultan appeared from me and mine. He wore Ottoman garb, of course, including a large bulb-like headdress. His robes were of gold and trimmed in red. He was not tall. In fact, I could nearly meet his level gaze. His skin was a shade or two darker than ours, but not drastically so. His beard was full and dark, extending to just below his neck. And he had the most peculiar odor. To this day, I cannot determine exactly what it was I sensed on that first encounter. And as the years went by, I truly did not notice it at all. Perhaps it was the simple smell of otherness, of people different than ourselves, who ate different foods, had different practices in day-to-day existence. Perhaps it was nothing more than a youth's hyper sensitivity to strange surroundings.

"May I present my sons," said Father. "Vlad and Radu." There was an unfamiliar quiver to his voice. Well, of course there was. He was in the process of betraying the flesh of his flesh!

"Vlad, yes, so lean, so intense, I see it already. And Radu. Ah, but you are a handsome one." Murad's smile was broad and false and even in these early moments I found a great dislike for the man. "Mehmed, would you please show the boys about the grounds? His father and I have much to discuss."

Murad's son, Mehmed, stepped forward, a wooden grin on his lean face. He was a handsome enough young man and, at least on the surface, friendly. Radu took to him immediately. And, yes, this is the same Mehmed who now holds me prisoner. The irony does not escape me.

Mehmed took Radu's hand and led us from the chamber and into the garden area. Murad had four wives and thus there were several children living on the grounds. Some of these were racing about the grassy garden and Radu immediately brightened. "Go. Play," said Mehmed. And Radu raced off with a giggle and a hoot. I, though, was not so pleased with the circumstance.

"We are not meant to leave, are we?"

Mehmed gazed down at me, his brown eyes dark and unreadable. "That is a strange question from one so young."

"I am young," I agreed. "But my father has made certain that I am well-schooled. I am aware of the practice of keeping offspring as hostages in order to ensure that the father does not renege on whatever pact is to be made."

Mehmed grinned. "Yes, young, but already wise. Things are likely as you say."

I did nothing then but to stare across the yard at my brother frolicking about with our sworn enemies. Already, I began storing up hate for the coming days.

***

I did not sleep much on my first night as a hostage. Our bed chamber was relatively spacious. We were well fed and treated like honored guests. In fact, during what was to be six years of imprisonment we were treated much as any other children about the place. We were educated in the native language, in the Quran and other significant writings. We trained in horsemanship and in the art of war. How foolish to train an enemy at how best to defeat you. Yet, in retrospect, both of us did not remain enemies of the Ottoman Empire, did we?

But yes, that first night. I have thought about it many times and can truly say I have never experienced the like since. Several times I have tried to dismiss it as the imagination of a frightened child. But the fact is, I was not frightened. As to my brother, oh Radu whimpered and squealed throughout the night. His sleep was restless and punctuated by waking terrors. But I, no, it was not fear that kept me up, for I knew that we were safe. What good, after all, is a dead hostage? To that end, what good is even a mistreated hostage? No, Murad had nothing to gain by our abuse. That would only give my father reason to refute their agreement and to storm the place with his men. No, what kept me up this night was not fear, but my first quite immature plans for revenge.

It was well past midnight when I heard the subtle flutter against the window shutters. At first I sought to ignore it. But whatever this was it was persistent, banging against the shutter repeatedly, squeaking in an almost language-like rhythm and intensity. Surprisingly, this was the one stretch during the night where Radu slept soundly.

After a time I tired of the racket. Rising, I moved to the window, staring at the locked shutter. We were situated in a tower some six stories above ground level. There were no bars on the window to keep anything in or out, only this flimsy wooden shutter that protected the room from the elements.

Tentatively, I reached out touching the wooden knobs that would open the obstruction. The commotion stopped. All was silent. Whatever was on the opposite side of the window knew I was there. I trembled. Of course I trembled. I did not know what awaited me. Perhaps it was a great hawk with hooked talons that could claw out my eyes and a savage beak that could bite my fingers clean through. It would not be the first time a person was attacked by such a creature.

But I was an impetuous boy, inquisitive and reckless. My curiosity had been stirred. Slowly, I drew back the shutters, both horrified and intrigued at what I might find.

A great bird hovered before me, its wings moving ever so slowly, just enough to keep it afloat. Never before had I seen such a thing. The size was immense as birds went, easily twice the size of any I had seen previously. The wings were broad and black as the midnight sky. And the eyes, they glowed red, a deep rich red such as blood.

For several moments we studied each other, this bird and I. My hands trembled to be sure, and my breath, well, I am not certain that I breathed at all during these eternal seconds. Yet there I stood, matching the creature's gaze. I could not fathom why it did not attack. Could it be that it feared me as much as I did it? No. Even at this young age I could sense that I was in the presence of a predator. This thing knew no fear.

A shudder raced up and then down my form as a peculiar mist rose about the thing. It was a clear night, not a cloud dotted the starlit sky, and yet suddenly, against all nature, this bitter cold mist rose to envelope the creature.

And when this devil's fog dispersed – for certainly Satan himself was in the origin – I stood before, not a bird, but a beautiful young woman clothed all in white. At first I thought it to be a wedding gown, but no, perhaps grave clothes. The fabric was shear, nearly transparent, and rippled in the subtle breeze. Her hair, dark and long, spilled over her breasts. Her skin was as pale as porcelain, but her eyes were alight with that same demon flame I had seen in the bird only moments before.

She hovered there. Just hanging in the air, supported by nothing more substantial than the lingering mist.

And she grinned such a sly and tantalizing grin. I was yet a boy, had not yet grown into manhood with its passions and indomitable urges, and yet my blood rushed at the sight of her. My skin flushed, my limbs tightened. A strange flutter danced upon my belly. My impulse was to step right through the window and into her embrace to be kissed by this magnificent woman throughout all eternity.

When finally composure settled upon me I asked, "Who are you?" Why it was this that I asked, I cannot say. It would have made more sense to ask, "How is it that you hover like the very clouds?" Or perhaps, "What are you, some creature from the depths?"

Her grin broadened, exposing prominent teeth, sharp and curved and unnaturally white. I believe she may have giggled as she said, "Invite me into your chamber and you will learn all you desire to know." Her voice was low, soothing, melodic, nearly mesmerizing.

I did not answer for fear that my words might betray me and beckon her just as she had bidden. Somehow I knew that this was the one thing I could not do. I must not agree to anything she requested no matter how insignificant.

She pouted then. "Oh, do you not find me desirable? Do you not want to know me, to love me, to learn the secrets of time without end?"

Still I remained stone-like, fearing for my very loyalty to myself.

She laughed, full and hearty. "You are just a boy! Just an insignificant cub. We will meet one day. Some distant day when you are a true man. And then you will know my eternal kiss."

Eternal kiss? Had that not been my own thought only moments before? How could she have known this?

She was gone then. Whisked away in her ghostly mist. And there I stood staring through the open window convinced that I had either just met the devil or perhaps experienced a waking dream. In either event, I have yet to witness anything such as this in all of the intervening years.

***

There are few specific events from my time as a hostage worth recording. In general terms, we were well treated and well educated. And while this lenient handling only fueled my loathing of my captures and the culture which they promoted, this had the opposite effect on Radu. Perhaps it is because he had been so young at the time of our taking. Perhaps, as I suspect, he was simply weak spirited. But with each passing year Radu became more like our heathen captures and less the proud Christian he was meant to be. Even so, in those early years I would not have believed it if someone had told me that one day Radu would side with the Ottomans and stand against his homeland on the battlefield. In these years I did not yet despise my brother.

One additional event from this period in my life bares recording. Murad had relinquished his title to his son Mehmed. I was perhaps thirteen years of age and Mehmed had decided to take us with him on some minor diplomatic call as a learning experience.

We had stopped to stretch our legs and to tend to bodily functions. I stepped away from the party as we were near the crest of a rise and was curious as to what lay below. Moving toward the edge I looked down upon a vast valley. At first I was unsure of what I was seeing, for down below was a row of perhaps ten to twelve poles of seven or eight feet in height, each secured upright in the fertile ground. They were evenly spaced, or near enough. Each had been carved to a sharp point at the top. And each bore a bloodied and dying man. Some were spiked through the belly, some straight on up through the anus. All wore the military garb of my homeland Wallachia. I had heard of this brutal form of execution, impaling, but had never before witnessed it. The Ottomans did not invent it, but judging from the scene bellow, they relished in it.

One might think that I would be repulsed by such a gross display of cruelty. But this was not my reaction. No, to me, I found it fascinating, this art of torture. The great finesse utilized in extending the agonized death beyond the limits of human endurance. There is a brutal beauty in the suffering of ones sworn enemy. And yes, I envisioned Mehmed on such a spike, and his father.

And so many more.

Letter from Johnny Van Helsing to Hans Van Helsing
October 28, 1929

Dear Uncle Hans,

I know you heard about Capone's little beef back in February. The Saint Valentine's Day Massacre they're calling it. They say Capone was in Florida when it happened, but everybody knows it was him that was behind it. Pa's been all balled up ever since, scared Capone will come after us if we grow our operation. But Capone don't even know we exist.

Our operation's not sitting pretty like Moran's was when Capone went after him. You know, we're doing okay, but small. Anymore, I'm thinking Capone, he needs to get taken down a peg or two. Pa says leave it be. We're jake. Capone doesn't barely know we're here and that's how we wanna keep it.

But, Uncle Hans, I got bigger plans for my future. I heard you talking with Pa last time you were here. You said you could supply us with more liquor if we could expand our territory. Capone's got plenty of turf. It's been over half a year since that Valentine's thing, but the heat's on for him. He's gotta watch his step, you know? Maybe it's a good time for us to make some kind of move. I don't think he'd even notice if we just pushed out a few blocks. I know Pa wouldn't want me even thinking this. So, don't mention anything – please!

That's about all, but I know you always wanna hear about the family so here it is. I've pretty much already told you about Pa. Ma's not doing so good. She tries, you know, to be the same old spunky ma for us, but I can tell she's struggling. Just the way she moves so slow and she's so pale, just sits there doing crosswords and listening to radio dramas. She says, "Johnny, stop worrying and live your life," but then she drifts off like she's, I dunno, just not there.

And Charlie, he's all wrapped up in that chest full a papers and books you brought last time you were here. He just sits in his room reading that stuff. And, do you know what's in there? A bunch of crazy vampire stuff. Dracula, like in that book that has Uncle Abraham's name in it. It's like he believes it's real or something. The other day I saw him holding this old worn out book. I don't even think the writing is English. He's just staring at the thing and mumbling like he's in a trance or something. It gives me the willies. I had to yell his name maybe four or five times till he realized I was there.

And what's more, Pa's got him engaged to this hot tomato, Mavis Chandler. You know, Pa's partner's daughter. She's a real looker, but Charlie doesn't barely notice her. I don't mean no disrespect to my brother, but something's going on with that fella.

Anyway, I gotta go.

Johnny

From the journal of Charles Van Helsing
December 18, 1929

This is not a good time to live in Chicago. Don't get me wrong. I love my city. But, here's the issue: the stock market crash back in October has everyone terrified. Already, businesses are closing, factories are laying off workers. Honest hardworking people are standing on street corners begging just to feed their children. Even with the extra income from liquor distribution Pop has been forced to close two of his five laundromats, and this less than two months since the crash.

Despite all of this, I'm consumed with personal issues.

On one hand, I'm obsessed with the Dracula journals. Even when at work, my mind drifts back to that chest and its mysterious contents. It's almost as if it's calling to me, as if it's grabbing me by the throat and dragging me back to that corner of my room to again dig through the chest, searching for some as yet undefined piece.

And once I discover that missing bit?

Truthfully, I don't know what it is or even if it exists. The issue is, I've become obsessed and I don't like it. It doesn't feel right and it's not like me to give up control.

The other overwhelming issue in my life is romantic in nature. And the problem looms nearly as large as the journals. The problem is simply this: I'm engaged to a beautiful woman.

I know you must be weeping for me already. Poor schmuck.

Mavis Chandler is the type most guys long for. Her shoulder length hair is golden blond, her lips are cherry red, her skin is soft and subtle.

That's all well and good, but I don't love her.

Not in the least.

Not even a little.

You see, this is to be an arranged marriage. I know, I know. The practice is archaic, but our fathers have partnered in the bootleg operation and neither fully trusts the other. Both men thought that if Mavis and I married this would serve as a mutual deterrent against betrayal. Neither man would make alliances with say, Moran or Capone at the expense of his in-laws. Family trumps money is basically the concept.

Great for them, I suppose.

I went along at first, but we're just two very different people.

Doubtful that it could really be that bad?

Here's an example.

Last evening Mavis wanted to visit a speakeasy. Now, despite the family business I'm not a speakeasy kind of fella. Strong drink holds no appeal and crowds annoy me.

But I played the devoted fiancé and took her to the place. The room was narrow, dark, and jam-packed. It seemed impossible to move even two steps without being jostled. A thick cloud of smoke hung about the room causing the air to taste like factory smog. A five piece jazz ensemble was situated to the left of the bar, which was fine. I love jazz and they played fair renditions of Louis Armstrong and Baby Dodds tunes. Men yelled and jeered, women giggled and bantered. To me it was chaotic. Soon we were standing with a group of her friends, most of whom I'd never met. The conversation went something like this:

"This is my fiancé, Charlie. Charlie, this is Pauli, Francine, Mickey, Thaddeus, and Hope."

"Oh, hey, how are you doing, bub," said Pauli, a tall lean fella with a narrow mustache, dark slicked back hair, and green eyes already glassy with drink. "How'd you catch you a choice bit of calico like Mavis?"

A choice bit of calico? Did he actually just use that expression I front of the women?

Before I could respond, Mavis chimed in with, "Charlie believes in vampires! Isn't that right, Charlie?" She gave her friends a knowing eye. The one that says, "I told you he was a sap." I guess the lesson is that I can't share anything private with the woman I'm supposed to marry. Besides, Mavis assumes that since I went to Yale I must be some egghead bookworm that has no use outside of a library. She's never taken the time to figure out who I really am and so assumes she's stuck with some tedious lump.

Offering Mavis a dagger glare, I said, "I'm doing research. There's really nothing to it."

"Vampires," laughed Thaddeus, a near twin of Pauli. "Do you carry a cross and garlic cloves?"

"Don't be silly. Of course not."

"Have you met any?" asked Pauli.

"Again, research only. The documents were a sort of inheritance." By this point I had the urge to hit someone, but kept my temper for Mavis's sake. One of the things she never bothered to learn about me is that I train with a punching bag hung in our garage. I've got quite a roundhouse and a pretty mean left jab for a righty.

"Are you one?" roared Pauli. "Let me see those teeth. I better keep Francine away from this fella."

Throughout the exchange Mavis and the other two girls laughed hysterically. Finally, once the teasing had subsided, Mavis said, "Charlie dear, my drink's empty. Go get a refill." After a brief pause, she added, "Go. Hurry now."

I took her glass, smiled, and said, "No thank you. Not thirsty." I then purposely released the glass, allowing it to fall to the wooden floor where it shattered.

I winked and then turned to leave, figuring Mavis could find her way home with her friends. Obviously, she had no more use for me than I did her.

From the journal of Charles Van Helsing
December 19, 1929

I decided to tell Pop that I'm breaking the engagement and so accompanied him and Johnny on some errands. We were walking back from the market. Johnny and I were carrying sacks of groceries, vegetables mostly, and Pop had stopped to gawk at a Studebaker parked in front of Lou's Diner. Johnny had his eyes on one of my former school mates, Kimberly Walker, as she strutted past on the opposite side of the street.

"You see her?" said Johnny with a sharp nod of the head. "She likes me, you know." He rolled a toothpick at the corner of his mouth, part of his faux gangster look. "She can see I have the goods."

I rolled my eyes. "She's my age, you idiot. She doesn't know you exist."

"Nah, you're thinking of the wrong brother," he said with a wink. "That's you that don't exist because you never poke your dingbat head out from behind those stupid vampire books."

To prove his point, he tipped his fedora toward the girl, nodded and winked. Kimberly giggled, blushed, offered a sheepish wave, and then rounded a corner and out of sight. His quarry gone, Johnny gave me a quick pat on the back and turned toward Pop. "What you got there, Pa?"

"Twenty-eight Studebaker," said Pop. "Look at the sharp lines on this beauty."

Johnny nodded and grinned, sharing his appreciation. "Slick."

Pop bent down, gazing at the dashboard through the side window. "Wouldn't mind taking her for a spin."

"Sharp grill," said Johnny, still twirling his toothpick. "It'd be swell to look under the hood."

"They make these babies just over in Indiana, you know. South Bend. Maybe a half day drive. I wonder if I could swing a tour of the factory sometime."

They fell into silence as they admired the car and so I took the opportunity to make my announcement. I'm not much of a conversationalist. I have no use for a long preamble or build up. I just say what I'm thinking. So I said, "I'm going to break the engagement. Mavis and I have nothing in common."

Pop gave me that look that said, "What malarkey are you spouting now?" and blew air out in a long frustrated hiss.

Johnny twirled his toothpick and said, "Pa, if Charlie don't want her I'll take her lickety-split." He gave me a playful elbow jab in the side.

"Charlie, listen," said Pop. "You're not doing this to be happy, huh? That's not what marriage is for. Look at me and your ma. You think we love each other much? I mean I like her well enough, but we do it because it's what you do."

I refrained from expressing just how incredibly stupid his logic sounded and simply stared at him.

Pop continued. "I know what you're thinking. If I didn't love her why did I marry her? Well, she needed somebody to watch out for her and I guess I needed somebody to watch out for. It made sense."

"Yeah well, Good for you. But I'm done with this."

"Seriously, Pa. I'll take Mavis," repeated Johnny. And then to me he added, "Give her a taste of a real man." He chuckled and elbowed me again.

I slugged him in the bicep. He winced and moved a step away.

Pop laughed. "Come on, Charlie. Listen, you're engaged. But last I looked you don't have the manacle on yet. What I mean is avoid setting a firm date. Maybe this financial thing will pass and we can get loose from Chandler's dough. But right now we need the cash flow. Anyway, if push comes to shove, you marry the girl. What's so horrible? She ain't bad to look at."

"Swell. She's good to look at. Ask her to marry Johnny."

"See!" chimed my brother, still rubbing his arm. "Just what I was saying."

It was then that the black Oldsmobile turned onto our street. It rolled slow. Very slow. Pop knew what was happening before it registered with me. "Johnny! Charlie! Down!" he barked. And then he was roughly pulling me down behind the Studebaker.

I think I stammered a half formed question, but Johnny was already answering. "That's Mo's Place. I bet those're Moran's men. Or maybe Capone's."

He was referring to a speakeasy run out of the basement of a flower shop and the gangsters Bugs Moran and Al Capone. The speakeasy was supplied by a modest bootlegging operation similar to our own. Johnny was suggesting that one of these major players was sending a message that Mo should either do business with him or lose everything.

Before Pop or I could respond, one of the Oldsmobile's back windows opened, a gun barrel was extended, and blasts of stuttering gunfire echoed off the brick walls. Windows shattered at the small flower shop as waves of bullets rained into the place. There were screams and shouts. Everyone on the street dove for shelter. But amidst the chaos I noticed something that disturbed me almost as much as the senseless violence before me.

It was Johnny.

The way he stared at the Oldsmobile, at the destruction and audacity. It was as if he was transfixed. It was admiration.

And then, that quick, it was over. The Olds raced around a corner and out of sight. But still, there was Johnny, staring at the scene with this goofy grin on his face, a toothpick dangling from his lips, and a gleam in his eyes. And I had a really bad feeling slinking across the pit of my belly.

Note from Joey "The Club" Rizzo to Al Capone
December 20, 1929

Boss,

I been checking out that joint on the southwest. Marty Martini's. They been supplied by a small time operator, Van Hessing I think they call themselves. What is that? German? Anyways, Marty, he seems smart enough. He don't want to risk getting you angered on account of him buying from the competition and what not. I made my point clear to him like I do. He saw the light. We can start supplying them next week.

So here I am in this joint and I overhear these two young punks at a corner table. It turns out they're with the Van Hessing operation. The younger guy, he can't be more than eighteen, he's all dressed up like you, trying to look sharp and all. He's saying the Van Hessings need to expand. They got to cut into your territory. The other guy, I'm thinking maybe an older brother, he don't seem too keen on it, but the young punk, he won't let it go.

I don't think it's anything big or nothing. They're a couple of kids. Small potatoes. Just thought you should know.

Club.

From the journal of Charles Van Helsing
December 21, 1929

There's something significant I've hesitated to commit to writing or to mention to anyone. The journal of Vlad Dracula, not my great uncle's translation but the original document written in Dracula's native tongue, the pages that he actually held, the pages he bled on. This document calls to me. I can't read it. I don't know the language. But night after night I find myself alone in my room, the lights out, the entire house asleep and there I sit stroking those centuries old pages. Often I have no memory of moving from my bed to where the chest sits, of retrieving the book, of the hours spent caressing it. I know you must think I've lost my mind, but it's important that I report these things as accurately as I can in case anything ever…

Well, I'm not sure how to finish that thought.

I was going to say, "In case anything ever happens to me," but I don't think that quite gets to the heart of it. I guess it would be better to say "in case I'm unable to give a true account."

Yes. That's better, I think.

I probably need to give you some context, so let me share my most recent, my most horrifying experience and then you'll either believe as I do or set aside this account convinced that I'm a lunatic. Maybe both.

Last night I came to my senses at nearly three AM. There I sat, on the floor of my bedroom, naked except for my underpants, my back against the plaster wall, covered in sweat though the room was chilly. But this apparent act of sleep-walking was not the strangest part of it. For all about the floor were houseflies. Hundreds of them. Big juicy horseflies as well as little gnaty things, various breeds, a fly menagerie. And all of them silent. Not a hint of the annoying buzz that normally accompanies these filthy little things. They weren't dead. They didn't seem impaired in any way. They were just silently watching me. All of them, just staring at me. Or perhaps staring at the journal that I held.

I gazed back at them, meeting their peculiar eyes.

I can't say how long I remained this way, but at the time it seemed eternal. And yet at some point, something changed. Somewhere in that infinite night I realized that the flies were speaking to me. All of them. Collectively. These weren't words. They weren't audible. It was simply that I knew what it was that they wanted me to do. What I needed to do. That this act was suddenly imperative.

I sat there, nearly naked on a cold December night, clutching the true journal of Vlad Dracula, the impaler, the vampire. Gazing at unreadable words in a language I didn't know. And there were blood stains on these pages. Brown with age, dry, crusty. It was Dracula's blood. I knew this. Dracula's strong undying blood.

The flies instructed me to partake of the blood.

The sacrament.

Blasphemy, surely. I'm not an overly religious man, but Dracula's blood, a sacrament! What words could I use? Heresy? Sacrilege? Take your pick.

I fought against this strange idea, to consume Dracula's blood. It seemed lunatic. Unforgivable. Certainly if there is a heaven and a hell I would be forever damned.

But the flies. This multitude of flies. Hundreds of tiny eyes staring at me, peering into my soul, pushing me, pressuring me. It was hard to think with all of those flies repeating the same thing over and over.

Partake of the blood. Partake of the blood, they said.

The flies were so strong. Their collective minds pressing, pressing. Tiny minds. No intellect to speak of. But together. So many together. And was there one other presence? Guiding, controlling, greater, yet thin and far distant. The message was beyond seductive.

It seemed my room, tiny to begin with, shrank to no more than the size of a closet. The walls nearly pressed against me, the cold breeze swept in through the window pane swirling about my limbs as if to embrace me in its cold deathlike arms. Only moonlight bathed the pages before me. My twittering hands clutched the journal. It wasn't a large book, maybe six inches tall and four inches wide, leather bound, black. The thought struck me that it looked very similar to a Bible. Well, maybe the Bible of the devil himself.

The pages were yellowed to golden, some to a rich ruddy brown. The blood had been spilt across the upper right corner and had proceeded to seep deeper into the pages. It was Dracula's journal, he carried it with him always, even when he died. Both times that he died. And this, this crusty brown matter, this scab on the page, this was his life's blood.

Life.

Yes, life.

I extended a finger, first tapping at the blood, just feeling it, exploring, like the first tentative kiss of new and unsure lovers. So cautious, so needy, so full of possibility.

Nothing happened.

I ran my fingertips across the page, caressing it, memorizing it, learning its topography, every fold, every bend, the indentations made by Dracula's quill, the rough texture of the bloodstains. Such beautiful script, forceful and sure, yet with subtly and dignity. Such rich golden leaves of varying hues. So enticing, the blood, the seductive life giving blood.

Gently, so gently, I scraped at the blood with a fingertip.

Partake of the blood.

It didn't come away at first. I scratched a second time.

There. A small bit of crust was now lodged beneath my fingernail like when I'd picked at scabs as a boy.

Partake of the blood.

I stared at it, studying it, amazed that this was actually the blood of Dracula darkening my own finger.

And yet, it was nothing special. Nothing dreadful. It was simply dried blood. Nothing to fear.

I can't tell you why I did it. It wasn't a conscious decision, just impulse really. But I put the finger in my mouth and sucked. My tongue danced across the nail, urging the dried blood from beneath, lovingly persuasive, drawing it into myself, onto my tongue where it tingled sweet and cool before sliding down my throat to where it settled into my being.

Such a strange thing to do and yet I felt no revulsion at the act. Excitement if anything. A thrill like I'd never known. My entire body tingled with static energy. I felt almost as if I should dance, or maybe open my window and yell out onto the streets, "I have eaten Dracula's blood!" But that would have been irrational. So I just sat, satisfied at one level and profoundly disturbed somewhere deep within.

And the flies.

How do I describe the flies?

There I sat, smiling stupidly, bare back against the cool hard wall, and the flies, still silent, none taking flight, came to me nearly as one. They simply marched forward, climbing first upon my legs, and then my torso and arms, and even onto my face and into my mouth and ears and nostrils. Hundreds of them, maybe thousands. All silent, all embracing me as one of their own.

I didn't cry out. I didn't try to shake them off or leap to my feet stomping and screaming. I simply leaned my head back against the wall, closed my eyes, and relished the sweet taste still tickling my tongue.

Three hours later I awoke in my bed. I was alone. There was not a single fly to be found. The journal sat innocently on my nightstand. Hurriedly, I reached for it, flipping through the pages until I found one where a small swatch of the blood had been scraped away.

It was true. It had really happened. My God, I thought. What had I done? What insane thing had I done?

From the journal of Charles Van Helsing
December 27, 1929

I think I might be losing my mind.

My mind! The one thing I've always trusted. Not only my intellect, but my determination, my resolve to walk my own path. My willingness to confound expectations: the intellectual who was also an athlete, the athlete that could care less about professional sports.

But, the journals, the writings – Dracula! It's all I can think about. It dominates me in ways I can't express.

I want to believe that none of it's real, but how can I deny what I've done. Eating chips of his blood! Something is happening here and it's either truly supernatural or I'm insane.

To complicate my day further, Mavis and her father, Earl, were at the house today. Pop and Earl needed to talk business and Mavis came along mostly because Pop told Earl that the two of us need to spend more time together. Earl's a small man and rather fussy. I guess that'd be the word. He's probably an okay fella but nothing ever seems just right for him. He has to add his own little change to anything Pop suggests. It's annoying.

As to Mavis, she was still mad at me for leaving her at the speakeasy a couple of weeks back. I was distracted by thoughts of Dracula's blood, but pulled myself into focus. I needed to maintain control of my life.

"You were with friends," I said in response to her complaints. "It's not like you had to walk home alone."

"You abandoned me – your fiancée."

I rolled my eyes. "You were doing your best to make me look like a sap. Be honest. You don't want to marry me any more than I want to marry you."

"So, what are you doing? Dumping me?"

I shrugged. "It's not dumping if it's mutual."

For some reason she couldn't see the logic in this and hissed, "If anybody dumps anybody it'll be me dumping you, Charlie Van Helsing."

I was fine with this. My ego could withstand the rejection, but I felt it prudent to keep that tidbit to myself.

Mavis marched into the living room, seating herself beside my mother on the couch. I sat to the other side of Mom. The exchange had taken place in the kitchen, and to my knowledge, no one had heard the argument.

Mom doesn't like Mavis much but goes along with the engagement because Pop says it's what's got to be. And since her illness, she just doesn't have the energy to fight it. But Mom could sense the tension between me and Mavis and so decided she still had enough spunk to make Mavis's visit just a little more awkward.

"Mavis, would you like some tea?" asked Mom. "No. Silly me. You're the kind of girl that always needs something stronger."

Yes, that was an insult.

Mavis, of course, is just as fond of my mother.

"Would you like me to help you with those dishes? Oh, you don't do them yourself, you have your sons do all the work. How many months, again, since you were cured of the pneumonia?"

Meanwhile, oblivious to the women, Pop and Earl were discussing business. Pop stood, arms crossed at his chest. "We need to be more cautious with deliveries," said Pop. "There's extra heat these past few weeks."

Earl was pacing back and forth, constantly pushing at his glasses with his index finger. "No, no. Well, not that it's not a swell idea, but…"

And there I sat.

Pop and Earl debating distribution, Mom and Mavis prepared to bring out the claws, Johnny was fortunate enough to be in school, and I was about to go insane.

Barely bothering to excuse myself, I rose, grabbed my jacket, and exited through the back door before anyone had much chance to object. I just needed to get away. It wasn't only the tense dynamics of the two families, it was more that I needed to think. Something has gotten into my brain. Something of Dracula and it terrifies me.

I wandered the streets, leaving the residential area and making my way into a commercial zone. Somewhere along the way I decided to visit a bookstore I'd passed many times before, but never had reason to enter. Mystic Pages was a corner shop tucked away on a narrow boulevard. The one story building was slender and of red and brown brick both inside and out. Hardback volumes both new and old littered half empty shelves. Strange mystical symbols adorned the walls. There was a mixed scent of old dusty tomes and some sort of sweet incense thick in the room.

A young Negro woman was carrying a stack of books to the counter when I entered. "Hello," she smiled, setting the heavy stack on the wooden counter before facing me. "Can I help you find something?"

I must have hesitated because her smile broadened and she giggled just a little. "Yes? What is it?"

She was beautiful. Absolutely stunning. Her skin was the color of midnight, her deep brown eyes rich with kindness. Her full broad lips dipped into a playful pout. "Hello?"

"I'm sorry. I just… The place is… different than anything I've seen."

I doubt she believed that the store was the cause of my sudden gawk, but she chuckled. "Come in. Browse. Is there anything I can help you find?"

I stepped forward, gazing about the place but still drawn to the sight of this beautiful young woman. What would Pop say if I brought a colored girl home? "Yes," I said. "I know this might sound strange, but I'm looking for information on vampires."

"You're in an occult bookstore. Very little sounds strange."

I nodded. "Fair enough. Vampires, then. Do you have anything?"

She grinned. "Just to be clear, you're looking for research material, not fiction like Dracula."

"Dracula's not fiction." The words were past my lips before I'd thought to stop them.

Her eyes narrowed, her smile reconfigured into something curious. "You're only the second person I've ever heard say that."

"Really? Who's the first? I might like to meet him."

"Turn around, then. I'm right here."

The voice was heavily accented. Nothing I was really familiar with. Something I would associate with an island people, I suppose. I turned. The man was sitting at a long table that was covered in books. He was nearly invisible behind the stacks.

"This is my Uncle Clyde," said the woman. "He's the house expert on anything supernatural."

"You believe the tale of Dracula to be real?" he asked. "Why?"

I moved toward him, coming to stand before the table. Like his niece, his skin was deep black, but his gleamed slightly of perspiration. His head was shaved to bald. His eyes were narrow and his mouth expressive. I don't know why I revealed this, maybe just to have some release of burden, but I said, "I have the original documents that Stoker used to compile the story."

His eyes widened. "And how did you come to be in possession of such a thing?"

"They were passed down to me, from an ancestor."

"Oh? And who is this ancestor that he had these documents?"

"Abraham Van Helsing."

There were several moments of silence as the man studied me. Finally, he said. "You must sit." And then to the young woman he said. "Pearl, you must join us. This, I think, you will find interesting."

Pushing books to the side so that we could speak eye-to-eye, Clyde said, "Let me tell you this first. I am not an expert on vampires. But I am a lifelong student of the occult."

"In Haiti," said Pearl as she claimed a seat. "Clyde was a bokor."

"I'm sorry. A boker?"

"It is nothing," said Clyde. "And it is in the past." His tone was one of irritation.

"He was the spiritual leader of his village," smiled Pearl. "And he was known to have great magic and was more prosperous than any for many miles." Here, she patted her uncle on the shoulder. He eyed her with loving exasperation.

"The point is," said Clyde. "I know many things, but do not specialize in vampires. Now, tell me about these documents."

We spent nearly an hour discussing the chest and its contents. Clyde was full of insightful questions and Pearl, though less knowledgeable than her uncle, was quite bright and contributed much to the conversation. She asked how my great uncle had come to know so much about vampires, a question to which I had no answer. She asked about Stoker, how he came to have the journals and if he'd presented them accurately in the novel.

"There are inconsistencies in Stoker's account," I said.

"Inconsistencies?"

"In Stoker's book, the few references to Dracula's past seem close but not a perfect fit to Vlad Dracula."

"Yes, yes, I have wondered this myself," said Clyde. "It is believed that the vampire Dracula is the same man Vlad III Dracula. Some name him Vlad Tepes which means Vlad the Imapler."

"Is that true?" asked Pearl. "Is this Vlad Dracula your vampire?"

"Absolutely. I have his journal. But Stoker's inconsistencies aren't in the original writings. It's almost as if he deliberately shuffled some of the details in order to avoid pointing directly at the true man."

Clyde nodded. "Maybe he was trying to give the impression that this was truly a fiction. Perhaps he feared that if the public knew too much about the true Dracula some fool would seek a means to resurrect him."

"Resurrect him? Is that even possible?" This, from Pearl.

"Perhaps," said Clyde. "But a terrible thing it would be."

We talked for another thirty minutes before I finally excused myself. Clyde's questions were becoming more probing and I was afraid that I might slip and reveal something about eating the blood chips. I felt comfortable with these people. Clyde was an unusual man, but kind, and I'd be lying if I didn't admit that I was taken with Pearl. But they were strangers and this was a secret I intended to carry to my grave.

In the end I promised to stay in touch and asked that Clyde contact me if he came across any vampire related materials that I might find useful. He smiled, clasped my hand, and said, "Take much care, friend Charlie. I fear you tamper with a danger you do not yet recognize."

From the journal of Vlad Dracula
circa 1477

It has been some time since I have made entry in this journal, though I have reread my earlier entries many times in the intervening months. It seems strange that I would choose to resume writing now that I am dead. For truly the things of life no longer interest me as they had during my living years. But still, I suppose it best that I summarize at least some of the events leading to my demise. If for no other reason than to offer context to the strange events that would follow.

When last I wrote in these pages I gave an account of my time as a young hostage to the sultan Murad, and soon thereafter his successor and son, Mehmed. I was released from my childhood incarceration after several years. Then, a young man, I returned to Wallachia to discover that my father and my older brother, Marcea, had been assassinated. The Ottomans had taken control. In a strange twist of fate, they offered me the throne. It seems in their minds, I was to be a puppet ruler. For they thought that my many years among them had turned me into an ally.

Though I readily accepted the throne and allowed them to believe in my compliance, I never once intended to serve their heathen schemes. I was resolute in my love of my country and my God. If anything, my time away had caused me to love them more. When the Ottomans taught me the art of war, I dreamed of seeking revenge on those hated foes. Thoughts of retribution drove me to excel in all that I did, whether it be physical prowess or book learning. I even learned some of the dark arts from these my enemies, the ways of alchemy and of strange supernatural rites. Oh, yes, this may seem blasphemous for I do claim Christianity as my faith, but all was done with the intent of one day eliminating these heathen from our land. And what more righteous cause could there be?

Not so, my brother, Radu. For he had become the traitor that Mehmed hoped me to be. He loved our captors and relished in their culture. He dismissed the land of his birth and the people that longed for his return. The Ottomans would have been better served to place him on the throne in my stead.

But, I would not maintain a longstanding rule. In total I held the throne three separate times during my mortal life and forever struggled against the despicable Ottomans and often against those of my own faith who had divergent agendas as well.

My practice of impaling enemies of the state became known far beyond my borders. And as a result, my subjects learned that I was willing to go to great lengths to protect them. Perhaps the most notable, or notorious, example of this is the time that some pompous sultan, I forget his name for he was insignificant, prepared to meet me in battle only to discover nearly twenty thousand of his subjects, men, children, women, all impaled upon large wooden stakes. Many were still living as my men had perfected the art of inserting the pole through the lower body and maneuvering around major organs thus allowing the subjects to remain alive for hours or even days.

I watched from a vantage above, convinced that this oaf would retch just as many of his men had done. To his credit, he kept his meal within his belly, but he did retreat, later issuing a statement that they could not capture a country run by a man so terrible and unnatural. Unnatural! No not then. And when later I would join an unnatural existence, it would be at the hands of Ottoman monsters and not of my own devising. It seems they made me into the monster they always claimed me to be.

Another notable event was my revenge on the nobles of Tirgoviste. These were the swine responsible for the deaths of my father and brother. To their amazement, I invited them to my castle to partake of the Easter feast. Certainly they wondered if this was truly an effort at reconciliation or if I had some devious plot to capture or murder them. To that end, they brought a full contingent of men. I welcomed them all.

We feasted long through the day, telling tales of battles and victories, getting drunk on wine, watching children both theirs and mine, frolic about the grounds. I wanted them to feel at ease, you see. I desired that their sentries relax, that there be a sense of goodwill.

It was near evening when finally I leaned forward, my elbows resting on the tabletop, a goblet of wine in my hand, and asked, "Did my brother scream when you buried him alive? Did he beg for mercy? Did ever his echoing cries wake you at night?"

Well, all of those seated about the table went silent. Mouths hung agape. One woman choked on her wine, spitting it onto the table with a strangled gasp. No one dared speak.

"Do you suppose," I continued. "That you should expect any greater mercy from me than you showed to my father and my brother? Do you think me so weak that I would forgive such an affront so easily?" I grinned, raising my glass in a mock toast. "Should we drink first to my father or to my brother?"

Already my men were in motion. The Tirgoviste troops were rounded up, the nobles protesting, cursing, begging for mercy, were bound and caged. The next morn my new prisoners were marched some fifty miles to Poenari where they were forced to build for me a mountain fortress. This, I believe, was truly a kindness, for I could have slayed them outright. As it was, most had several months of life before the fortress was complete and I impaled the surviving members of the party.

Certainly, these actions might cause some to think me evil. After all, I ordered the brutal executions of children and of women. Clearly I must have a damaged soul.

This, I assure you, would be an unfair characterization. Did I desire to murder children? Of course not. Those children were innocent, their souls beyond reproach. But the difficulty arises when one remembers that children become adults and that innocence is left behind, even scoffed at and ridiculed. Tell me what would happen to a child who knew that his father and mother had been impaled? Or of a child that learned that his mother died as a slave building a fortress for her sworn enemy? Would not such a child grow into a man set on revenge? One must remember, we are at war. And not a war fought solely for gain of land or riches. These Ottomans seek to unseat the very foundation of our culture and to force us to worship their foreign god. We fight for our identity as a people and for the God which we serve. With such incredible stakes at risk, how could any true leader do anything less than to defeat such an enemy by every possible means?

Were these children and women innocent? Yes. Of course. And no, not in the least. Did they not worship the heathen god? Did they not cheer for their menfolk when they won battles against my beloved Wallachia? And did this not make them enemies? I am not proud of all that I have done. But I do not have the luxury of regret. I held a responsibility to my subjects, and for them I would commit even the most vile atrocity, even to the damning of my very soul.

And so it would seem this has occurred.

But as stated earlier, these concerns are for the living and are no longer my burdens to bear. Already, stories have spread concerning my demise. Some suggest I was slain during a simple hunt. Others say I was butchered by corrupt Wallachians disloyal to their crown. Most say I was killed in battle. This, I suppose, is the closest to the truth. But allow me to tell the tale as it actually occurred.

It was a winter's eve, cold and blustery. Yet, the battle continued even as the sun sank behind the horizon. I was weary. My limbs ached, my great longsword was heavy in my hand, and my steed was slow and clumsy with exhaustion. Still, the battle continued. And I, as the prince, had no choice but to set the example. Urging my weary steed onward, I charged a group of foot soldiers, my blade held high, a savage war cry bursting from my lungs.

I slew two of the Ottomans on my first pass. But as I turned to reengage, an arrow sliced through the air striking my mount in the chest. The horse faltered, took three hesitant steps, and then tumbled sideways onto the frozen ground.

I managed to leap free of the beast, avoiding the danger of being pinned beneath the dying creature. Recovering my fallen sword, I met the group of foot soldiers on level ground. Battle fever overcame me and my fatigued limbs were reinvigorated as I charged into the mass of blades and flesh. I was as a wild man, slashing, screaming, cursing. One man, brutishly large but slow to respond, was down nearly before it began. With a mighty yell, I moved to the next man, bringing my blade down, but it was blocked by a thick two-handed sword. The man was strong and his blade sturdy. I pivoted, avoiding a slash from another foe situated to my far right.

Blades swished, sparks danced from the bloodied steel as time and again metal met metal. Two glancing blows found my left arm, but neither penetrated my mail sleeve. I swung and parried, jabbed and dodged. My opponents were closely grouped, which hindered their mobility, but I too was at near quarters and equally inhibited, though not by fear of striking an ally.

I felt a sting in my left calf as a narrow blade penetrated a gap in my armor just below the back of the knee. I whirled, striking the man who had injured me at the base of his neck. He tumbled forward clutching his damaged neck, not yet dead, but out of the fight.

I was struck again and then again. Now, I was forced backward. I was a competent warrior, superior even, but even the best fighting men may become fatigued and I was weary and facing uneven odds. My hand trembled as I clutched the hilt of my blade. For the first time I wondered if perhaps this might be my final battle, that perhaps I'd just witnessed my last sunset.

Another step backward and I tripped over the huge brute I'd felled two minutes before. Laughing, my foes moved toward me as I frantically twisted about, attempting to rise before they were upon me. I was better than this. I would not be felled while thrashing about on the ground like some fledgling bird fallen from the nest.

But, then they stopped, eyes wide, all of them to a man. They saw something, I knew not what, perhaps a wolf or some other predator coming up behind me. And then they were stationary no longer, but fleeing as rabbits into the brush. I forced myself to my feet and spun about to see what it was that I faced. The sight was as nothing I had seen in life.

Women.

At first I saw only four, but soon I realized that others were emerging from all sides, perhaps a dozen of them in total. Some were dressed in gowns such as one might wear at a banquet. Others wore what could only be called rags. Each glided across the ground as if their feet evaded the surface. They were Ottomans, all of them, I could tell this by facial structure as well as clothing. But they were unnaturally pale, none bearing the rich deep skin tones of their race.

And their teeth.

Oh, mighty God in heaven, their teeth.

They moved slowly, studying me like the predators that they were. One appeared from behind a nearby tree, two more from my right. Some smiled, others simply stared expressionless. One whispered in another's ear, like a lover sharing a forbidden secret. These two shared a girlish giggle. Each made eye contact with me, a deliberate connection as if they were peering into my very being. The eyes were strange, glowing. I'd seen eyes like this only once before, on that first night as a hostage to the Ottomans. It was a memory which haunted me still.

One woman moved forward, an eager grin on her crimson lips. She glanced at each of her companions. There was a nod, and then they moved toward their prey.

I tried to fend them off with my sword but it was knocked from my hand with the ease of an adult slapping a stick from an infant's grasp. I struggled, punching, clawing, kicking, even biting. But they were upon me now and there was nothing that I could hope to do.

I cannot tell you where first I was bitten for truly it seemed they all descended upon me as one. There was the neck, the torso, the thighs, the arms, buttocks, feet, hands, truly it seemed that not one area of my body was ignored. There I lay on the snowy ground, my armor ripped from my form. These savage beasts were draining me of my life fluids and still I screamed and thrashed as if I might some-how resist this inevitability. But I was becoming weaker by the moment, my vision becoming dim, my limbs no longer responding to my commands.

And when it seemed my light was so dim as to evaporate into vaporous mist, when all was lost and no hope remained, then came the strangest act of all. A tall willowy woman with long black hair trailing nearly to her hips pressed her face to mine. With curved talon-like nails she ripped away the flesh of her neck. I resisted as she drew my lips to the cavernous wound, but I was spent, no natural strength remained.

She forced me to drink.

By all that is holy, she forced me to drink!

Truly, I thought I would retch as the blood spilled past my lips and into my mouth. But from the first it was the sweetest wine I'd ever known. I drank hun-grily, ravenously, greedily, filling my belly with life-giving fluid. As soon as I'd taken all that I could from one woman, I was passed onward to receive from another and then another.

But, this was not yet my birth into the eternal midnight. This was merely the conception. First I need die in order to be born anew. And so, after I had drunk my fill, receiving from each of these miraculous creatures, the first woman, the willowy one, approached me. Her name, I would later learn, was Sevda, and she drew me to her, running her tongue across my lips, tasting the remnants of blood that remained there. She kissed me, long and erotic. And then, without word or even change of expression, she slashed my neck wide with her nails and dropped me to the snowy ground where I died.

From the journal of Charles Van Helsing
January 05, 1930

I've swallowed flakes of Dracula's blood on three more occasions since my last journal entry. I can't tell you why. There's no thought to it, no logic, no secret desire. It's something that just comes upon me, almost like there's another mind manipulating my actions. As you might expect, this disturbs me. A lot. But I can't control it. When the desire flares, all self-will disappears.

Worse yet, there's no one that I can talk with about this. At least no one that might listen without sending me directly to Sigmund Freud's couch. I could talk with Johnny, but he'd just tell me that I was loony and then go back to impressing his pals with his junior gangster status. Pop's not an option. He'd just call me a sap. Mom has her health to worry about. I certainly shouldn't add stress to her life.

It dawned on me that maybe I should go to the book store, to maybe ask the Haitian Clyde for his help.

As soon as this thought occurred to me, I grabbed my overcoat and rushed from my cluttered bookkeeping desk at the laundromat and made my way to that little brick hovel of a shop.

I could see Pearl through the front window. She was moving back and forth, cleaning the place, a smile on her face. Beautiful woman, just beautiful.

And there was Clyde, sitting at the table, studying some old tome, just as he'd been on my first visit. It was almost as if he'd never moved. It was such a serene moment, something I so wished to join. Something so welcoming but still so distant.

But then Pearl glanced toward the window. Her face registered something, maybe recognition, maybe even joy at seeing me.

I don't know why I did it, I'm not a fearful man and I don't run from social confrontation, but I turned and hurried away. There was no reason to fear these people or even to be embarrassed. But I simply couldn't allow this secret to be revealed. It was almost as if something prevented me from stepping through that door, something foreign, something not of me.

Now I feel more alone than ever. Clyde might be the only person to take this seriously enough to help me, but if I can't get past these impulses – this influence – enough to ask his help, where do I turn?

Letter from Johnny Van Helsing to Hans Van Helsing
January 17, 1930

Dear Uncle Hans,

I got so much to tell you. Big stuff. But, well, I guess I need to start with Charlie because I think once I get onto the business stuff I'll forget to tell you about my brother and that's important too. Besides, it all kind of slides into each other anyway.

So, Charlie was in another one of his moods, just sitting there in his room staring at that old book he got out of that chest. So, I was coming to tell him about my plans because I wanted him involved. But it's like he was blotto or something. I kept trying to get him to talk and he just stared forward like, well, staring. Finally I knocked on his nightstand with my knuckles. The same way I would if I was knocking on a door. He didn't move. Not even a blink. So, I did it again. Nothing. So, you know, I smacked him on the back of the head. That got him.

I asked him, "What you doing?"

He said, "Nothing."

Well I can tell he don't even know how it was I found him sitting like that. But he's all serious like he just lost his wallet or something so I said, "You're a knucklehead. But you're my brother and you got me worried. Tell me."

He shook his head. I slapped him on the cheek. You know, playful slap. Normally, he'd tackle me after that, we'd smack each other around a little, then he'd tell me what was rattling around his noggin.

Nothing like that this time. In fact, he didn't even react at all.

"Hey," I said. "You okay? You're not acting like you should."

Nothing. No response. Now I'm really getting the heedbie-jeebies.

"Is it Ma? She's going to be okay, Charlie. I can feel it." This isn't true. If anything, Ma's slipping, but I needed to try to brighten Charlie up and was thinking maybe this was why he's in the mopes.

Still, nothing. So, I put my hand on his back and we just sat there for two, maybe three minutes. I didn't say anything because I figured he ain't ready to talk.

37

Finally, he looked at me and said, "Johnny?"

"Yeah," I said. "You got me worried. What's bothering you?"

He thought for a minute. You know, like maybe he wanted to tell me something, but wasn't too sure he should. To my utter dumbfoundment he looked at me and said, "I've eaten something evil."

"Bad grub? That's all that's eating you," I said, thinking all along that I'm glad he didn't say he thought he was a vampire because Charlie's obsessed with this vamp thing and as far as I can tell, I think maybe he really believes in monsters.

He looked at me like maybe I didn't understand what he meant and then bam! He goes back to staring at that dumb book. As if I wasn't even there. Just, click, off goes the light switch. What were you thinking, by the way, giving him all that stuff in the chest? You ruined the guy, Hans, honest. You ruined him with that stuff.

So, I shook him a little, just to bring him back to earth. He looked at me and I figured we needed to talk about something, anything. You know, get his mind off that book. And the whole reason I came to his room was to get his help on my little project, so I pitched it.

Well, now Charlie was back from Neverland. "Johnny, no. Absolutely not. You could get someone killed."

I shook my head. "No. Honest. I got it all figured out. Nobody gets hurt."

We argued for a while, him asking me details and then shooting everything down the way he does. I said, "Just because you're older don't mean you know more than me."

He said it does. We argued some more. He said, "Johnny, think about Mom?"

"What do you mean?"

"If something happens to one of us. In her current state that might kill her."

This made me stop and think for a minute. I wouldn't admit it to him, but he was probably right. But I had this all worked out, and besides, I'd already recruited some fellas from school, you know, my pals. I promised them a cut and so I couldn't turn chicken. So, even though he'd stuck this Ma thing in my head, I said "I'm doing it anyway. No one'll get hurt. But if you're so worried, help me out. You know it stands a better chance if you're my right hand."

He cursed a little – and Charlie never curses. But of course he agreed I'm right that it stood a better chance with him in the mix.

So, here's the deal. Remember how I said I thought we should maybe cut into just a little corner of Capone's operation? Well, I got a friend who has a friend. He said to me, Capone's got a shipment coming through on Thursday night. He tells me the road they're going to use and there's a stretch before they get into the city that's pretty deserted. Not much traffic, not many buildings, no lights to speak of. I mean, that's why they take that route, right? They don't wanna draw attention.

So, I figured we'd ambush the shipment. Just set up a road block, get a few guys with some Tommy guns I quietly borrowed from my buddy Louie's pa. Now, these guys making the delivery, they don't wanna die for Capone. They don't want any hassles, just make the delivery and be on their way.

And here's the thing, nobody ever needed to know we were the ones that did it. We get some extra product and they get a little dry spell in this neck of the woods. So who do you think Capone's clients will turn to if he ain't got his shipment for them?

That's right. Yours truly.

So here's how it went down.

We had eight of my pals and we had five Tommy guns. Enough to make an impression.

So, then I could see the headlights coming up the road. We had two trucks facing each other. These blocked both lanes. My guys were in the bushes on either side of the road. Me and Charlie, we were standing right there in the road in front of our two trucks. I had a Tommy gun, Charlie was unarmed on account he was still protesting this thing.

So, the Capone truck rolled to a stop. This gorilla type stepped out of the driver side. He wasn't carrying any heat that I could see, but I didn't trust what I was seeing, you understand.

I nodded to my guys and they stepped out from the brush.

Gorilla guy, he looked at them, smiled, nodded. Then he gawked at me. His eyes narrow like he was studying me or something. "You're the Van Hessing kid, right?"

Well, I'm dumbfounded. He said the name wrong, but he knew us. How'd he know us? We ain't that big.

"Yeah. I seen you before," he said. "You're in way over your head."

So, here's Charlie whispering in my ear. "Johnny, walk away from this right now."

I knew better. We walk away now we walk away with bullets in our backs. We had to play this through. "You seem to know me," I said to gorilla guy. "How come I don't know you? I guess you're just a pion, you know. Just the delivery guy."

"Johnny!" hissed Charlie. "Have you lost your mind?"

"The name's Club" said gorilla guy. "Now, you gonna call your kindergarten troop off or are we gonna have a real problem?"

"I have no problem," I said. I was thinking what's one shipment to Capone? The guy's worth millions. Club probably won't even tell him about this. Why would he risk getting Capone all angered up at him for losing a shipment? They'll just absorb the loss. No one loses.

Club chuckled. "Oh, you've got a problem little big man. You got a real problem if you don't let us pass."

"This ain't worth dying for," I said. But the truth is, I was sweating piss.

"No. It ain't," agreed Club. "You might want to keep that in mind. You're young. You got some guts. Now how about you prove you have some brains."

"We'll leave," shouted Charlie.

"No we won't," I yelled. "I don't know who you think you are, Mr. Clubby. But you're not the guy in control here. You got that?" To be honest, I didn't know what I was doing. I was just flying by the seat. Charlie, he tried to step up, to take charge, but I just kept talking right over him. He still didn't get it. "Now, here's how we're going to do it," I said. "You're going to tell your guys to stand down and then you're going to unlock your truck. After that, you and your men are going to load the hooch into our truck, this one here." I pointed at the one to my left rear.

Club smiled. He said, "I'll tell you what. The way I see it we could fight it out here and we'd come out on top. I'm certain of it. But fellas on both sides would die and you see, I don't want to lose no men to a punk like you. So, yeah, Van Hessing, you win this time. I guess that makes you feel good, huh?"

I tell you, Uncle Hans, I was scared out of my head right then. But we got the hooch and here it's been over a week and nothing's happened. Me, I think Mr. Club was just saving face in front of his fellas, you know, he couldn't show just how scared he was. Pa still doesn't know nothing about it, so don't tell him. Charlie's angry as a cat after a bath, but I think he's keeping his mouth shut on account he don't wanna upset Ma. Business is good. Everything's jake.

So that's about what I have to say.

Regards,

Johnny

From the journal of Vlad Dracula
circa 1477

The telling of my awakening may be somewhat scattered as I did not enter into my new life with much in the way of cognitive ability. My first memory is of coming to consciousness in a dank musty dungeon strewn with hay and dirt. I was near naked, my clothing in tatters. Amazingly, a few of my possessions which I'd carried on my person had been kept with me, this journal among them. I later learned that allowing me these few familiar items was done in order to aid me in regaining my memory and, more importantly, my right mind. For when first I rose into the eternal midnight I in no way resembled the well-educated and cultured prince that I had been just three days before.

Someone had tossed soil across my chest. This dirt, I would later learn, was of my homeland and thus carried certain nourishing properties on which I would depend. Once educated in such matters I would take to carrying a small pouch of the stuff with me at all times along with this journal which had been bloodied during my death. This blood – my blood – I would learn, might well prove to be a life sustaining gift at some later point, and so, like the dirt, will always be with me. In truth, I have peppered some of the dust of my land throughout the pages so that this one leather bound account might forever sustain the life of he whose tale it tells.

I was a beast. There is no plainer way to say it.

I had no memory, only vague flashes of shadows and horrors. I did not have language or understanding or reason. I was pure instinct. Ravenous. Angry. Confused. Growling and hissing. Loping about my small confined cell. Sniffing at the strange and revolting odors. Beating my fists against the walls. Racing to and fro.

My senses were enflamed. My vision was crisp, sharp, able to make out every distinction. Though the flickering torchlight from the corridor beyond my cell was minimal, still I could see every divot and hairline crack in the thick stone walls. I could perceive the delicate patterns on a fly's wings though it hovered in a dark upper corner, its wings flapping furiously. How was it that I could make out such detail?

My sense of hearing was overwhelming. Voices, even whispered, I could hear, and the gurgling of water, this at least a mile distant. Livestock and carts and wind and birds and war. I could definitely hear the clash and clamor of war in all of its beauty and brutality.

My skin was sensitive to even the slightest variable. I felt the shifting of fabric against my flesh, the textures of each length of hay on which I lay, I could actually feel the air movement caused by the fly's wings.

And smell. Certainly I perceived odors from miles distant: mud, grass, men, women, livestock, vegetation, decay. All of these assailed me. And yet, decay was the overwhelming odor. I could smell the rotting corpses of vermin from within the walls and of prisoners whose bodies had been carted away days or even weeks earlier, of birds that perished on the parapets above. It seemed the overwhelming fragrance of the earth was of rot and deterioration. But most disturbing was that I could smell decay on my own form. As if I myself was a dead thing!

All of this, as amazing as it was, amounted to nothing more than a tickle at the back of my mind, for my first thoughts, if they could truly be considered thoughts, were of thirst. And this thirst was like nothing known in the natural world.

I needed blood. Living blood, drawn directly from the veins of one still alive. The sense of it was overwhelming. My stomach twisted, my throat tightened, my mouth was dry. Even my limbs quivered.

I created a great commotion, vocalizing wildly as I stomped about my cage, tossing hay to rain down upon my head, and charging at the iron bars which held me captive. Again, again, I charged these metal obstacles, slamming my frame against them, shear animal panic rising in my breast. Truly I was as any caged beast. My instinct was to flee this cage, to break free, and to seek prey, to feed on the flesh of another.

***

It seemed an immensity of time, but in retrospect I believe Sevda came to my cage almost at once. Likely she'd been waiting for me to wake. She was quite tall, slender, with long black hair. Her cheek bones were high and caused curious shadows across her dark luscious skin. Her eyes were deep and dark, with a peculiar, almost red, glow to them. This glow, though barely perceptible, was striking and fierce, and somehow comforting. She spoke to me, but in those moments the words were only random sounds, for my language skills had yet to return.

But it was not her words that captured my attention. For with her was a human girl. Just a child showing the first hints of womanhood in her boy-like figure. Sevda opened the door to my cage and pushed the whimpering child forward.

I needed no instruction in what to do. I was a creature of instinct and so fell upon the terrified girl with animal lust. She screamed of course, but her cries were cut short as I fell upon her, my newly-formed fangs sinking deep into the soft warm flesh of her neck, ripping, gnawing, devouring. I had no skill, no finesse, no compassion for my human sustenance. I had need and that need was all-consuming.

I drank deeply, feeling the luscious warmth of the living blood course through my form. How marvelously sweet. How comforting. I cannot express the rich beauty of this first experience. This was so much more than food. So much more than a mere means to survive. This blood vitalized me as no mortal shall ever understand. And I found that I wanted more, so much more.

When finally I had drained the child of all that her body could deliver, I dropped her to the ground like the empty sack of flesh that she had become. And I gazed upon Sevda with a leer. She returned my grin, adding a throaty chuckle. "Oh, my fierce cub, you are a natural." She strolled forward extending her arms over my shoulders and locking her fingers behind my neck. "You will be a strong one," she added. "Very strong. Very desirable." Here she teased her tongue across my still bloody lips, again offering that throaty chuckle. "Very desirable."

As I said, I was a creature of pure instinct. And so, like the animal that I had become, I responded to instinct alone, satisfying my needs to the fullest as I drank of both her blood and her passion.

***

Sevda became my tutor in the ways of the vampire, teaching me how to draw blood with subtlety, even keeping a victim alive if I so chose, instructing me on our limitations, of what dangers might befall us, of the dangers of the sun, and of garlic, and so on. She was at once a companion, a mentor, and a lover. Always she called me her fierce cub which, in truth, grated me, for no matter how new I was to the eternal midnight, never would I be a mere cub. It did not take long for my earthly memories to return for it seemed the more human blood I consumed, the more humanlike I became. Not that I would ever be truly human again, but my language skills returned along with my memories and I became less the beast and more the man.

As well, I found that my physicality had changed somewhat. Obviously there were the fangs. These were the most notable change. Long, curved, and terribly sharp. But my hands and feet went through a metamorphosis as well. Where once my fingers had been long and slender, now they had become thick and stubby. My palms and the pads of my feet had small tufts of wiry hair. I also found that my physical strength had doubled, perhaps tripled.

My first true hunt took place some few weeks after my awakening. Some language skills had returned by this time, and along with them, some rudimentary memories. But I was still as a child, or better, as a trained pet. We came into a village sometime after midnight. Most villagers were indoors, asleep, their homes secured. But nighttime is the hour of the scoundrel, and so these we found readily if not in abundance. Mind you, we had no qualms about feeding on the good-hearted. The blood of the innocent is as sweet as that of the rogue. It's just that the decent persons are rarely about in these hours.

Sevda and two other females, Devlet and Hafza, led me through the shadows. "Stay with me, my cub," instructed Sevda.

Hafza offered a prolonged purr, then said, "Look at him, how eager. He is a fine specimen. I might just devour him myself." Grinning lasciviously, she licked her lips, slow and sensuous. This one was a hellcat, and quite appealing as well. But I was distracted. Never before in my new existence had I strode the streets of the living and so had little interest in my vampire companions, no matter how enticing. The scent of pulsing blood was overwhelming. How was I to focus on Sevda's commands with distractions on every waft of air? I could hear the beating of hearts and the rush of precious fluids through the veins. I could smell the exquisite nectar of life and the sweat that oozed from the pores. And this not only from those willing to brave the night, for I could also collect scents from bed-chamber windows, from inns, and stables. From all about me.

I had not yet attained many of the higher abilities my kind might gain over time. I could not control small creatures, for instance or call a wind or a mist. In truth, I did not yet know these things existed. And so I hunted only as a beast hunts, first smelling my prey upon the midnight breeze, and then hearing the subtle breathing, and eventually coming to within direct sight.

As my three female companions moved toward a clutch of whispering men clinging to the shadows just outside of a large estate, I moved in a contrary direction, as I had caught a whiff of blood that called to me. I slipped between many small homes and stables along the uneven lane. The night was cool, the sky clear, allowing a three quarter moon to bath my path with golden light. My target's footfalls echoed in my ears as I slinked about in the shadows. A man and a woman together. She smelled of fear while he smelled of lust. The man was tall and stern with the beginnings of a widening belly. His face had a splotchy aspect to it and his nose was red with drink. The girl, though, ah the girl reminded me of my dear wife Ilona, a stout woman, but comely with dark brown hair, nearly black, a regal nose, and narrow intelligent eyes.

Before that moment I had not remembered Ilona. She had been as so many other things, simply a vaporous shadow dancing about my mind. But here, now, I remembered her as well as my offspring, Mihnea, Vlad, and Mircea. Here, I experienced what must have been my first true pang of emotion since awakening to the eternal midnight. I remembered courting Ilona while still a prisoner of Mehmet. Of walking through the gardens hand-in-hand, of subtle kisses and energetic lovemaking. I remembered the beating of my heart within my chest whenever she would smile and the cool sweat on my palms as I held her hand for that very first time. I thought upon a summer afternoon with my son, Vlad, of giving him his first sword, instructing him in how best to defend himself against a larger opponent. These memories rushed through my mind in a whirl of intensity and then fled before I could truly grasp their significance. For the thirst was upon me, and no amount of sentimentalism no matter how profound could distract me from my true purpose.

I was upon the couple with the stealth and speed of any great predator. The male I dispatched with cruelty and rage, gouging his throat to lay bare his veins. The man was so startled that he had little chance to scream before my savage fangs nearly ripped his head from his torso, but the woman caused enough commotion for both of them. Realizing that her shouts would awake the village, I turned to her, dropping the lifeless corpse of her would-be rapist to the hard cold ground.

Sevda had taught me that we have a means to command the mind of our prey and here I practiced this for the first time. I moved closer to the woman, my eyes fixed on her own, our souls locked in some eternal moment. Her expression went slack, her posture relaxed. Her entire world now consisted of my eyes and my desires. Such a curious sensation to tickle another's soul, to dance about the corners of this woman's mind to nettle and direct. It seemed as natural a thing as breathing and yet simultaneously ghastly.

"Ilona," I said as I moved to her. "Ilona, my love." Truly, these sentiments were fragments from another life and I was hardly aware that they had been spoken. The woman was beautiful to behold and her resemblance to my earthly love only compelled me further in my bloodlust. I growled, low and menacing, a guttural tone rising from within my chest. Her skin was soft to the touch, her pulse strong and fast with fear. I smiled. "Hello, my delicious dear. Hello."

My fangs sliced through tender flesh. She released a subtle sigh that resembled that of passion. Her blood was warm, sweet, full of life and vitality. I had to control myself for I did not wish this to end too soon and so I attempted to ease the flow of the succulent fluid. I so wanted to preserve this moment, to drift in this ecstasy with this nameless lover forever onward.

She offered another sigh, this one long and wispy. Her legs quivered as her life's fluid drained from her form and so I lifted her into my arms, never once releasing my precious kiss of death and life. This was pleasure beyond any I had known as a man. Her fluids filled me with warmth. My limbs quaked with building energy. It seemed I might burst in some pinnacle of elation. Oh how I wish the girl could have lived throughout the night to share in this delicate dance until the sun chased us into our graves.

She gasped, a hint of a grin tracing her now-cool lips. I released my hold on her vein long enough to gaze down on her face. "Ilona," I said. "Sweet Ilona." And then I finished the deed.

Her heart ceased beating with such subtlety that I nearly failed to recognize her passing. I gazed upon her still white form and saw nothing but a dead thing. Any resemblance to my past love had fled with her life. This was now a husk, nothing more. And so, the spell broken, I tossed it aside as one would any refuse.

Disgusted with the two rotting forms at my feet, I quickly found my way back to my female companions and discovered that they had, with vicious efficiency, dispatched the group of scoundrels that had been casing the large estate.

Sevda grinned at me, her face still gory from the feast, her cheeks flushed pink with stolen blood. Hafza glided to me and began to lick the fresh blood from my lips. She cooed and nibbled as she undulated against me, tracing her fingers along my chest. I celebrated with them long through the night in a hedonistic romp of fleshly indulgence. But something had changed within me. My feelings toward these beasts was not as it had been prior to this eve. Where even an hour before I would have reveled in every moment, now I went through the motions almost mechanically, fulfilling my expected role, but taking no great pleasure in the act.

I had crossed a threshold of sorts. With each day my memories became more vivid and soon I was fully aware of the man I had once been, of the family that I had lost, and of my countryman that I had failed. And with this awareness came the realization that Sevda and her companions were of my hated enemies, the Ottomans. And how I loathed the thought that I had lain with these filthy creatures, shared my blood with them, received this eternal curse from their very veins. Even more disturbing was the thought that I may have been brought into the eternal midnight for a purpose. That perhaps my enemies were utilizing these children of darkness to do their bidding.

By this point it was common knowledge that I had been slain. Several men had claimed responsibility for the act. Some poor soul who had the misfortune to resemble me had his head placed upon a stake and displayed as proof of my demise. But, what would happen if I should reappear as a monster, wild in the bloodlust, savaging my own people for need of the precious nectar? Oh, I could see the plan clearly enough. They would imprison me, starve me perhaps for weeks before releasing me onto my own people. I would be crazed and beyond rational thought. How the Ottomans had initiated a deal with Sevda and her ilk, I cannot say. Perhaps they promised the vampires free reign in Wallachia if only they would leave their homeland free of their kind.

It is all speculation. But the more I dwelled on these thoughts, the more certain I became. Could it be coincidence that I, the prince of Wallachia, had been the sole man taken from the battlefield by these creatures and made to be one of them? Could it be coincidence that they were, to a one, Ottoman by birth? No. This I could not believe. I was a prize to them. I had been their prey, not by random choice, but by design. These creatures hunt regularly, but I have yet to see them bring another into the eternal midnight. Why then did they do so with me if not for some greater aim?

And so I began making plans of my own. Sevda was my tutor in the ways of the vampire and now I became a student as never before. I probed with questions, often causing her to pause as if wondering at my aim.

"Why do we shun the sun?"

"For fear of death," smiled Sevda, for the question likely seemed remedial.

"Obviously," I replied. "But what is it about the sun that causes our death?"

Another time I asked, "How many ways are there to slay our kind? Tell me of each."

Throughout it all I kept the pretense of fellowship within this coven of vampires. But this was a strain, for with each passing night my revulsion grew and the thought of laying with such as these revolted me to nausea. Still, I had a purpose, I had a scheme, and in order for me to succeed, I must play a part.

***

One night, perhaps six months after my first hunt, we came across a burned out village, strewn with bloodied bodies. Small fires still burned. Scavengers pecked and tore at dead flesh. Sobs could be heard by survivors who curled up in doorways or laid in the street weeping beside their dead. The place had been the scene of battle this very day. Along the main pathway stood several large poles, sharpened at the tops. Each pole held the victim of impaling, many were already lifeless, but some agonized souls still cried and moaned in horror and pain, their bodies ravaged. Though I had become known for this particular means of execution I had learned it from the Ottomans and had taken it up largely as a means of using their own savagery against them.

And now I knew what it was that I would do.

Now I had a plan.

I must pause here to note that I had gone through many changes in these few months. Sevda in particular was amazed at my growth in what she referred to as special abilities. Though she was my mentor, Sevda had hidden many things from me. I had not been instructed in how to control the creatures of the land with but a thought, or of how to crawl along an outer wall as might a lizard. And yet, these abilities I had obtained without instruction and apparently much sooner since my rebirth than was common. I do not know why this should be so. Perhaps the fact that I had been both bitten and then made to drink from so many different vampires on that awful night, that I had received the gifts of a dozen seasoned creatures and not but one, contributed to my accelerated capacities. Perhaps it had something to do with my own human makeup, of my natural fortitude and intellect. Whatever the cause, I found that even as a babe amongst my companions, I already had attributes surpassing many of the others. These I would use on this very night.

I knew not when another opportunity such as this would present itself. Nearly our entire assembly of vampires hunted this eve. This happened occasionally, but it was not the daily practice. Add to this the opportunity to utilize impaling, and I took it as God's design that I should act.

The prospect of slaying nearly twenty of my kind in one bloody battle was daunting; for obviously once I'd made my first move the rest of the hoard would converge upon me with little mercy.

But, no. I was approaching the problem with false assumptions.

I was thinking as if it was I alone against twenty, where this was not truly the case. I'm certain that a wicked grin creased my features as I closed my eyes, attempting to send my commands to the hundreds of tiny minds creeping about the ravaged village.

I saw only minor movement at first, a skitter here and there, a pair of beady black eyes and then another. I could hear them well before I could see them, my army assembling. The trick would be in keeping my foes unawares. Most were feeding off of the poor souls who had been unlucky enough to have survived the military action. The greater part of my mind still focused on my larger task as I growled lustily, tearing into a nearby human with a gusto often reserved for the larger jungle cats, making such a commotion as to distract my companions from the more subtle sounds of my assembling brigade. I tore the man's throat open, drinking in a gurgling frenzy. Tossing the still-living man aside as I then launched myself upon another. Delvet and Hafza were sharing the blood of a young woman not thirty feet away. Both glanced up at me, offering bloodied grins. Hafza winked and then licked her lips. No, you vile sow, you would not have me for your pleasure this night.

I could feel them now, my army, still growing steadily and now anxious for my next command. I could not wait long for some among the vampiric number would surely sense their presence. In life I had been many things, a prince, husband, father, a philanthropist of sorts. I had also dabbled in alchemy and other curious distractions, but always within my soul I was a warrior. I was the leader of men upon the battlefield. And this was the aspect of which I now operated. This would be a glorious battle.

With a savage roar, I called my army of vermin forward. Seemingly hundreds of them appeared from cracks and crevices, from atop buildings and amidst the trees. Rats, mice, cats, birds, stray dogs, horses, even a pair of wolves, all were suddenly present. As one they sprang upon my former companions, chomping, gnawing, pecking, biting. The screams of the astonished vampires were deafening.

I saw Delvet fall beneath a fury of rats, each clawing at her, nibbling her dead flesh, picking at her. A male vampire, Yazid by name, was crushed beneath a charging steed. Another was fighting off a dozen birds. Already, they had pecked his eyes from the sockets. No, these creatures did not have the ability to deal death to my kind but they could inflict significant pain and occupy my former companions while I went about my work.

My window of opportunity was a small one. The vampires are a strong breed. Some had gifts similar to mine and these would seek to gain control of the beasts. I needed to act while they were too preoccupied to pay attention to my actions.

Hurriedly, I rushed to my right, snatching the seductive Hafza away from a hoard of mice and rats to carry her in my arms as one might an infant. "Dracula," she gasped. "What has happened?"

Clearly she thought me to be rescuing her from this madness. But I said nothing until I had marched across the field toward the nearest impaling pole where finally I said, "Justice, you Ottoman sow. It is justice which has descended upon your foul coven." Before my words could fully register, I lifted her above my head and brought her down upon a five foot tall stake. The force of the thrust pushed the sharpened end all the way through her from back to chest and pressed the corpse already occupying the pole nearly to the ground. She gawked in shock at the bloody wood protruding from her own form.

Her eyes met mine. She attempted to speak, perhaps to say the word, "Traitor." But she had not the breath. In the end she simply spit on me and then died.

And then the most astonishing thing occurred. Hafza's form shuddered violently, and then cracked in several places, splitting and popping, before crumbling into dry gray dust. Amazing. The process took less than a minute, half of that even. Only a few bones remained to remind me that only seconds before this had been a living, sentient being.

But I had no time to ponder this and so grabbed another of my kind, the nearest at hand, and performed the same grim execution. This one decayed but a little, appearing as a corpse might after two or three years in the grave. Curious.

I repeated this act again and then again until, after five vampires in various degrees of decay dangled lifeless upon wooden poles, a cry went up. Several vampiric heads turned at the sound. "Betrayer!" was the cry. "The fledgling has betrayed us!"

The attack had now been seen for what it was and even as my army of beasts persisted in their attack, my former companions moved toward me. A large male, Sunduk by name, was the first to reach me. My strength was the greater and yet he managed to hold me long enough for two others to approach before I disposed of him by breaking his neck. Still, vampires are a hearty breed and Sunduk survived the injury. His head dangling at a hideous angle, he continued snapping at me even as others grabbed my limbs to begin shredding the skin from my bones.

As stated, I am quite sturdy even among vampires, with skill surpassing those of most of my kind, but my strength and my abilities are not infinite. As my flesh was pierced my concentration wavered and, suddenly leaderless, my army of vermin fell away. I was now overcome by vampires and knew that certain death was but moments away.

It was then that Sevda came forward. Her lower lip had been chewed away leaving only a jagged flap. Words slurred, she said, "What have you done, little cub? Do you not know of the plans I had for you? Do you not realize the gifts I have given to you?"

There seemed to be genuine regret in her tone and for a moment I felt a pang in my heart. I had not loved her, if such is even possible within our kind, but we had shared something. And I cannot deny that I felt some indefinable connection with her. As to her statement, I was not certain if my seemingly enhanced abilities had been a gift from Sevda. She was quite gifted herself and I had drank deep from her several times in those early days. Or perhaps she referred to the "gift" of the eternal midnight. If so, this was no gift at all. Regardless her meaning, despite our somewhat tender beginnings, I had come to be repulsed by her kind and had nothing left to say to this foul thing.

I struggled and bit and clawed. I was a cornered beast and would not be taken easily. I ripped the ear from one of my foes and bit the nose from another. I kicked and scrapped, howling like a wolf and roaring like a lion, inflicting much damage on my adversaries but still I could not break free.

Sevda stared at me, her eyes dark with emotion. It seemed she wanted to say more, and if she had, if by some fluke she had shared some tenderness or genuine emotion, perhaps I would have regretted my acts, perhaps I might have even conceded. But her face hardened and she looked away from me saying, "This one is called the impaler. Very well, then. Impale him."

A roar of celebration went up as I was hefted from the bloodied ground and moved toward the nearest impaling pole. Struggle as I might, I could not loose myself from so many strong grips. Panic filled my breast. Though I loathed what I had become, though I detest this dead and yet living existence, I found that I was not prepared to relinquish it easily. I kicked and spat, clawing at those nearest me, biting any flesh within my reach.

High above, hovering about the trees, I heard squeaking and the subtle flutter of leathery wings. I cannot say why these sounds stood out amidst the chaos surrounding me, but they captured my attention. Looking toward the sound I saw three bats fluttering about. Such beautiful creatures. Sleek, mysterious, free of man's tampering. If I could but fly like these, I might be free as well.

If I could fly.

If I could be as the bat.

I don't know that these were intentional thoughts. Perhaps it was some deep instinct bringing forth an as yet unknown ability. Perhaps my sheer concentration amidst terror for my very existence enhanced or modified some as yet undeveloped characteristic, but I felt the most peculiar surge ripple through my body. It began as a nauseating tingle and built into a blinding pain. Something was happening within me and certainly my captors sensed it for they dropped me, nearly releasing me in unison, leaving me to writhe about on the ground pitching and clawing. Tufts of hair pressed through my flesh in dark gnarled clumps. The bones within my limbs shifted with loud cracks and pops, seemingly shrinking as they rearranged their configuration. There was a moist sucking sound from within my chest. I doubled over, the pain in my belly indescribable. I was shrinking. How could this be so? What purpose could there be? My arms became heavy and awkward which caused me to glace at them. To my astonishment broad leathery wings had grown. I recognized them as the type I'd seen on the bats far above. What foul thing was happening? Had not these Ottoman fiends done enough? Was I now under some new and devilish spell? But I did not have time for panic. I was surrounded by foes. And as my body continued to transform, I came to realize what had occurred.

I had wished to become a bat, and so the thing came to pass.

Not having time to contemplate the ramifications of this strange occurrence or even to question if I truly had the means to take flight, I forcibly calmed myself. I could not panic. I could not allow raw emotion to hinder me.

Within seconds I fluttered free of my still startled opponents. My vision was still clearing and my limbs protested their unfamiliar form and use. The process had not been instantaneous, but neither did it take as long as one might expect from such a complete transformation.

By Hell and Heaven both, how could this be happening? My mind was ablaze with questions and, in all honesty, a considerable dosage of fear. What had I become and was there a means to return to some more humanlike form? Was I now destined to spend eternity as a base creature? I cannot say with certainty that I have ever been so fearful and confused as in those first few moments.

My foes jumped and growled, attempting to swipe at me with talon-like fingers. None took to flight in pursuit. None seemed capable of this astounding feat but most were swift of foot and capable of panther-like leaps and bounds. If I had not risen quickly I might still have been recaptured.

I circled for a few moments, gaining some small measure of coordination. Eventually I spotted Sevda amidst the clamoring crowd. I cannot tell you why it was important for me to deal with this particular devil, perhaps it was because she had been the one to lead the charge in ripping me from my human existence, perhaps it was because we had known each other so intimately in these fierce days, but I could not flee without first tending to her.

Swooping down, I grasped Sevda's head in my claw-like feet and lifted her from the ground. I had no way of knowing if my new form would have the strength for such a task, if my claws could bear the weight, if my wings had strength enough to lift her humanlike form. It was a formidable task indeed, but I proved capable.

It was then that I perceived a shifting within my grasp, a flutter of movement, a change in density. Risking a glance at Sevda I realized she was in the midst of her own transformation, that I now clasped the head of a great night bird such as I had seen on my first night as a child hostage. Could this be? Could it have been Sevda all along? Had she selected me when I was a lad and then sought me out decades later? So many questions and no opportunity to learn the answers. For now Sevda pecked and clawed, fluttering furiously, pulling and twitching. Twice I nearly lost my grip, and so, despite my shock and curiosity, I made for the nearest impaling pole, swooping down, down, forcefully driving her head firmly onto the cruel and bloody stake.

It took less than a minute for her to return to human form. The point pressed upward from the soft flesh just below her chin through the mouth and sinus cavity and into the brain. Her body convulsed for several seconds. Her eyes locked on me and it seemed there was an effort to move her jaw. Perhaps she wanted to ask me why, or maybe to continue her tirade. Perhaps these were simple muscle spasms. Whatever the case, the pole had penetrated the brain and had likely savaged it to mush. Sevda would never again trouble me.

It was a grizzly sight and it would be untrue to say that I felt nothing. I loathed this Ottoman whore and yet she had been my closest companion in this new existence. And now it occurred to me how utterly alone I had become. For in no way could I return to my earthly family or to any other aspect of my former life, and clearly I had eliminated any bond with my fellow creatures of the night. Such a peculiar empty feeling, unlike any victory I had known as a mortal man. It was nearly as if I was the defeated instead of the victor.

And so I fluttered off into the night, still astounded at this newfound talent and newly fearful of the desolate eternity before me. Near sunrise, I found a shallow cave and dug into the ground, burying myself some four feet below the surface. This would serve as my grave for the daylight hours. Beyond that, I did not know what I would do or where I would go.

Letter from Johnny Van Helsing to Hans Van Helsing
February 3, 1930

Dear Uncle Hans,

I don't know how to say this. I don't really know how to say nothing right now.

Pa's dead.

There. I said it. I know I ain't done a good job of saying it nice and making you feel okay about it, but that ain't my skill.

It was Capone. It had to be, at least. It's not like anyone else would gun a guy down like that in the daylight and all. Pa was just walking into the laundromat with me, talking about Ma's coughing fit last night and saying he needs a hot cup of coffee. Regular stuff. Just another day. Then we hear this car speed up behind us and before we could even get turned around, it was over. Pa's on the ground bleeding all over the sidewalk and I'm standing there watching the car race around the corner and gone. That fast. Done. And Pa's dead.

I know this is scattered and I apologize and all that, but I don't really know what to do from here on out.

Ma, she's crying all over and oh, Hans, she's so frail. I don't know what to do for her. And Charlie. God, I don't know what to say about that guy. I mean, he says it's my fault, because of that raid and all. And he's right. It is my fault. And that's something I'm going to have to deal with. But, Charlie, he just sits in his room. He won't help me with Ma. He won't help me figure what comes next. He just sits there with that old book from the chest. It don't even read English or nothing. I don't know what it is with him. He won't talk. Just mumbles nonsense over and over. The guy's gone completely batty, and I don't think he really gets how far off he is. I need him now. But right now, when I need him most. He's just gone.

I guess that puts me in charge. I mean, Pa, he always said he wanted me to take over someday, that Charlie had other ideas for his life, and that was all well and good. But, I mean, Uncle Hans, I'm seventeen, you know. I mean, I'll do what's got to be done, but I wish Charlie, you know, was in his mind and all.

I'm sorry again, to tell you all this like this, but I don't know how else to tell it. I could use you now. Really bad, I could use you. Maybe you could make another trip this way sometime soon?

Johnny

From the journal of Vlad Dracula
circa 1485

Though my mentor has been gone these many years, my skills in the ways of the vampire continue to grow. I can now transform into a bat or into a wolf, or, should I choose, a number of other beasts, with little discomfort. I have learned that I might, to some small extent, influence the weather, causing winds and fog to rise as if from nowhere. My form can lose its solid aspect allowing me to move about as might a mist. This, I admit is quite taxing and the process is not near as complete as it might seem to those who witness it, but it is a useful skill.

Also – and this somewhat to my shame, for I was a man of faith and shunned such things in life – I have consulted with practitioners of the dark arts as a means

THE DRACULA JOURNALS: Dark Decades

of learning more about my peculiar condition. As such, I have learned many interesting tidbits, including a means to resurrect a slain nosferatu, or vampire as we are more commonly known. Even this very volume, I have sprinkled with many substances, among them my own vampiric blood and soil from my homeland, that these pages may aid in this endeavor. I should hope that there never be occasion for such a thing, but in the event that such is needed, the following procedure should suffice.

[Note from Abraham Van Helsing: Here, I purposely exclude the remainder of this entry from my translation as these words contain information that is affront to both God and man.]

From the journal of Vlad Dracula
1491

Why do I waste my time on you, God? Why do I bother? For so many years I have sought your comfort. Oh, true, I have played the part of the demon for certainly this is now my nature. I have slain without compassion. I have defiled the innocent as well as the scoundrel. I have relished in the misery of others and have drank deep the fluids of life.

But how can I be blamed? Did I ask for this fate? Did I seek it or beg for such a curse?

I tell you no.

And have I not, through it all, sought your grace? Have I not petitioned you for relief from these unholy traits?

And to what end?

For now I find that the very symbols of the faith have power to undo me.

Am I so unclean that the very cross of our savior should burn as a blacksmith's iron upon my flesh? Have I been so thoroughly rejected that all which is sacred is now accursed to me?

And for what I ask? Is this curse upon me alone or upon all who walk the eternal midnight? I wonder, if I should choose to make more of my kind, would this same jinx plague them? Would they shrink away from the holy symbols as I do? I think they would. But then, would Sevda, if she should yet live, fear the cross as I do? She was a heathen even before the damnable curse of the vampire. I suppose she already reviled the cross. Certainly, one such as her could find no favor in it.

Again I must ask why this fate has befallen me.

Did I not serve you in life? Did I not slay thousands of heathens in your name? Did I not ravage Ottoman villages, slaying man, woman, and child, preventing these from encroaching upon lands claimed in your name? Did I not honor your name each time I spilled heathen blood?

And yet this is my reward!

Damnation upon the earth.

Am I not even worthy of Hell? Is this my compensation for a lifetime spent in service? For this was not what I envisioned as I impaled thousands of your enemies upon bloody stakes of wood. This is not what I sought when I executed those who blasphemed your name or brought to rubble your cathedrals.

Oh, I suppose you will claim that these things were done for my own glory, that I used your sacred name to further my own earthly goals. To this I say nay!

Did my victories serve my earthly kingdom? Of course they did. And what of it? If perhaps I gained either position or notoriety, was this not done in your name? Did I not deserve some earthly increase for my efforts?

Apparently not.

For you have left me with less than nothing. I cannot even claim that my soul is still my own for my actions are driven by these unholy desires. And so I leave this upon your alter. I, who was by blood of the Order of the Dragon, I who was sworn to war for you and you alone, now renounce my faith. This is your doing. I am finished. No longer will I seek you. No longer will your name ever pass my lips save as a curse.

From the journal of Vlad Dracula
1581

Everyone that I knew in my earthly life has now gone to the grave. Ilona, my children, friends, advisors, all enjoy their eternal reward.

And yet I am here.

I have watched them each over the years, from a distance of course. Never did I allow any that knew me in life to see the despicable thing that I have become. In truth, within a few short years of my "death" it seemed each had all but forgotten me. My children grew and produced offspring of their own who then produced yet another generation. Wallachia proceeded as if I had never been. It all seems so useless now, the fighting, the death, the sacrifice. Did any of it matter in the least?

Letter from Anne Van Helsing to Hans Van Helsing
February 5, 1930

Dearest Hans,

I know you and Johnny are pen pals and I'm sure he's already written you concerning Vince's murder. That's not why I'm writing, so save your sympathies. I wouldn't want to hear them anyways. And please stop calling on the telephone. I won't take your call so don't waste your time. Hans, I just don't know what to say to you except that I wonder what goes through that bullheaded brain of yours. First, you drag Vince into that ridiculous bootlegging business and then you give Charlie Abraham's chest. We both know what's in there and we know what it was doing to you. What possessed you to give it to my boy?

Your harebrained bootlegging scheme has already cost me my husband and now Charlie's obsessed with those despicable documents that ruined Abraham's life and nearly did the same to yours. I can't say anything to him about it without giving away what I know. And if I did say something it would only make him more inquisitive. He's a private young man. Strong but quiet. And curious. Always curious. He's the type that keeps to himself, but I know he's caught some of the influence just like you did. I just can't say how much. There are changes in him, that's for darn sure. He's normally a very focused young man with goals and plans and the like, but now he wanders around like he's in a slumber. I don't like it. And, don't let my ill health fool you, I'll come right across the ocean and give you what for if anything happens to my boy, don't you doubt it.

Well, I guess that's most of it. I don't really know much about Vince's murder, but I can tell you right now, the boys likely know more than what they're telling me. They're protective that way.

Now, if it's all the same with you, I think it'd be just as well if you kept yourself on your side of the Atlantic for a spell. You've done enough damage if you don't mind me saying so.

Anne

From the journal of Vlad Dracula
1602

For decades I have moved about, hunting this village or that, settling for a time in one region and then another, never lingering long in any one area for fear of discovery and capture. On some few occasions I have come across others of my kind. These encounters are often typified by mistrust or even outright hostility. It seems only the nosferatu made by one another move together as clan or coven, that we do not trust those from another maker.

To that note, one event is worthy of note. Some fifty years after my rebirth into the eternal midnight I came across Sevda. Yes, somehow she had survived her execution. Likely one of her comrades had lifted her from the impaling pole soon after I'd fled the scene. I found her in a small outlying village feeding on livestock.

When first I picked up her scent, my heart quickened. Here was one I knew. Here was someone with whom I could commune. Certainly she would forgive me the transgressions of my early days. I had been foolish then, still full of patriotic pride and religious righteousness when I decimated our coven. How rash of me to have thought these nosferatu to be in the service of the Ottomans, for what care did they have for the politics of the living? I had been, as she had called me, a cub, irrational and fueled by misunderstanding and naiveté. She would understand that the decades had washed away my childish notions, that we could once again hunt side by side as we had done at the first.

But as I approached I saw that she was a mindless thing. I may not have slain her on that awful night, but I had stolen what minimal happiness she may have yet enjoyed. Rising from her position beside a slain cow, she stared at me, her eyes dull with confusion, her head cocked at an unhealthy angle, her tongue lulling from the corner of her mouth like that of a lap dog. Did she in any way recognize me? I cannot say. Perhaps some vague recollection, nothing more.

"Oh, Sevda," I said, emotion choking my words. "This is what you have become."

But she did not reply, for she was incapable of language or of any higher thought. She was naked and filthy, her body crisscrossed with scars. The blood of a dozen kills clung to her flesh as she shifted from foot to foot, nervous and unsure.

"Dear, Sevda. I am so sorry that I have brought you to this. If only I had possessed even a measure of wisdom I would have set aside the loyalties of my former existence and embraced you wholeheartedly."

She grunted and drooled and then gazed longingly at the lifeless beast beside her. This may have been Sevda's form, but any trace of intellect had fled long ago.

I slew her then, once and for all ending her suffering. She did not fight me as I drove a jagged length of wood through her heart. She did not reject me as I offered a simple parting kiss upon her forehead. She was ready for the end. Her simple mind may not have recognized this, but certainly whatever fraction of a soul remained had welcomed this long overdue conclusion. As I left her, I found that a strange emptiness had settled within me. Perhaps for the first time I realized just how lonely I had become. But I would not dwell on this, not for several decades at least. For the time, I simply moved on and then moved on again and then again.

But now I tire of this vagabond existence. And as such, have taken steps to secure for myself a permanent residence. One of the particular talents given me is the gift of mind-to-mind influence. The simple sharing of blood grants me the ability to transfix a human being, to make suggestions which these persons will then carry out with nary a thought. As such, I have influenced a certain solicitor. And, in doing so, have obtained documents identifying me as one of my own descendants. This same influence has allowed me over time to accumulate substantial capital. I now have both a title, that of count, and wealth. I have chosen to purchase land in the region known as Transylvania. It is a neighboring region to Wallachia, one which I had visited within my daylight existence. And thus familiar and comforting.

From the journal of Vlad Dracula
1603

I have purchased a castle in a sparsely populated Transylvanian sector. It is remote enough to offer privacy, but near enough to outlying villages to provide me sustenance. It is a large edifice, with numerous rooms, high gothic ceilings, and a substantial stable. Located high atop a rise, it meets every requirement and has given me a stability that I have not known in over a century.

It is also a lonely place.

It is strange, I suppose, to think that a nosferatu might feel a human emotion such as loneliness, but it is true. I do not know if I am capable of love or any true affection, but I most definitely crave the presence of another.

As such, I set about in search of a bride. I will bring another into the eternal midnight for it is time to share my existence with another, if for no other reason than to aid me in maintaining some semblance of sanity through the innumerable and insufferable nights.

From the journal of Vlad Dracula
1603

Her name is Lavinia and she is beautiful.

Her skin is soft and rich of color, her hair long and dark as was both Ilona's and Sevda's. She has a full curvaceous form and a saucy grin which seems to settle near to her right cheek when her mood turns to mischief. Her nose is petit, her large brown eyes glint with fire and vigor in the moonlight.

She was a tavern girl serving drunken laborers in an outlying village some fifty miles distant from my estate. I sat alone at a corner table watching her glide about the place, gracefully deflecting groping hands with a wink and a playful rebuke.

When finally she made her way to my corner, she grinned saying, "Do you partake of brew or of the vine?"

Returning her grin, I said, "My thirst is great, but I do not believe your establishment offers my particular vintage."

"Well, if it is a meal you desire, Olaf has a hog roasting on the spit."

"Oh, that a hog would sate me. But, no. Tonight it is companionship I desire."

Here, her smile fled. "Oh! It's that you crave! Well, I am not a trollop. I need the coin as much as any poor girl in this godforsaken place, but I get by well enough on my earnings, thank you."

"I mean you no disrespect, dear girl. It is no mere romp that I desire, but a true companion, someone to share my eternal misery."

I am certain this statement confounded her. Certainly, it was unlike any proposal she had yet been offered. "What does someone like you want with a girl like me? I see how you're dressed. You're no commoner and your accent is of another province."

I shrugged. "Titles and lineage no longer mean to me what they had in another time. That which I desire has more to do with the spirit of the person. And this I see in you."

That saucy grin crept onto her cheek. "Oh, you do, do you? Well. My spirit tells me you just might be trouble. What do you say to that?"

"I would say that you are perceptive beyond your years and that if you are satisfied with your current circumstances then you should walk away from me this moment. But, if you desire something more, something dangerous and forbidden, then you should allow me to take you from this place. But, know this, should you choose to travel my road you will never return to this place or to the people you know and love even if you should live a thousand years."

She stared at me, that twist of a grin dipping into a modest pout. "You're serious," she said at last.

"Most assuredly."

"And you want to take me where?"

"Why, to my castle, of course." I suppose I was playing the imp, but I find so little joy in this existence, it felt good to simply release myself into playful foolishness.

Here, she giggled. Certainly the thought of a castle seemed preposterous to one such as she. "And you don't want to hurt me?"

"Young woman, I do not desire you harm, but the truth of the matter is that I will most definitely injure you, even unto death. But this I promise you. If you agree to walk my road you will live into the next century and likely the next after that."

"That makes no sense."

"No. It would not. And yet it is true."

She cocked her head, again offering that so wicked grin. "You are dangerous, aren't you?"

"More dangerous than any you have encountered in this life."

"If I was smart I would have you ejected from this place."

"It would be foolish to do otherwise."

"And yet..."

"And yet you will come with me. And you will leave this life and all of its trappings behind forever onward."

I drove my carriage perhaps ten miles up the dirt road, situating ourselves between two villages. She cradled next to me in the seat and I could feel her pulse racing with misgiving. And so I took her chin and turned her head to face mine. "My kiss is not like that of any you have met before," I said.

She nodded, but that saucy attitude had fled into the cool night air.

"You are frightened," I said.

She nodded, still silent. I could feel her shudder.

"As well you should be. But you have committed to this course and it is beyond the time when I would allow you a change of heart."

I tilted her head, firmly grasping it in my hand. She gasped as I opened my mouth, revealing my so white, so sharp teeth. She jerked sideways, attempting to pull away, a confused flutter of syllables spilling from her lips.

I penetrated the flesh of her neck. She tensed, her fingers clutching my arm, her legs jittering against the carriage seat in a fitful rhythm of terror.

Her blood was warm and rich and I drank deeply. Never before had I drunk with the intent of cursing another with the eternal midnight, but in those moments I wondered why I had waited so very long. As Sevda and her companions had done with me on that first eve, I then offered her my own blood.

She fought this at first, pulling her face away from my offered wrist, where I had bitten deep to offer her access to my fluids. She whimpered and squirmed, but in the end she drank deeply. Once it was clear that this was how it was to be, she gave herself over to me in full.

Oh, what a glorious time we had.

From the journal of Vlad Dracula
1747

As previously recorded, Lavinia was the first of my nosferatu brides. We spent nearly a century, the two of us, partaking of villagers, drinking deep and lustily before returning to our residence to wrestle in fleshly passions throughout the endless nights. And for a time she satisfied me with her quick wit and endless desires. But, spirited as she was, Lavinia was a simple girl. She could not fully appreciate the finer things of life. She had no taste for the exquisite or for the philosophical.

Perhaps I make excuses. But the end result is that I eventually tired of her. I had no desire to put Lavinia out or to dispose of her in some crud manner. I simply brought another bride into my home. And then yet another. This displeased Lavinia of course, but there was little she could do. I, after all, was her master in all things.

Still, none of these women could fulfil the vast and widening vacancy within my soul. I do wonder if this is an element of the curse, that I will forever be unsettled, never fully content either in circumstance or within my own bosom. I suppose I could seek yet another bride, but if three cannot sate me, what could I expect from a fourth?

And yet, something must change. I cannot yet determine what that may be, but for now at least my only true joy is in the drinking of blood. And this I do in abundance.

Letter from Hans Van Helsing to Anne Van Helsing
February 13, 1930

My Dearest Anne,

I am so sorry. You cannot know the pain I know. Though I suppose you do not care, no? You blame me. I blame me also. But what can a man do? These things. These beastly things. How can I describe? I thought maybe the distance from here would lessen the curse, but no. That is not the real reason. A hope, yes, but not a reason. Fear and self-loathing, they were my guides and yet still they remain and so I have accomplished nothing. One advice I offer is to let our good Charlie be, no matter what you suspect. To interfere could be deadly. Allow the curse its whims. But then, perhaps my counsel is false. Who can know? Forgive me if you may. I have nothing to add and much to regret.

Hans

From the journal of Vlad Dracula
1889

I have decided to leave Transylvania. I tire of the place. I tire of the Szygany gypsies, of my lofty hideaway, of being feared and avoided. I desire a fresh environ. Someplace foreign and thriving. A place where I might simultaneously blend in with the masses and yet live the privileged existence I both deserve and crave.

I have determined that London England could be such a place and have thus been studying the language for several years. My vocabulary is now nearly that of a native, but I fear my pronunciations will give me away as a foreigner, and this I cannot have. For I must be free to move among the people, to interact and socialize in anonymity and to then hunt without fear that something as simple as an accent may give me away and lead enemies to my door.

From the journal of Vlad Dracula
1889

I have secured the services of a British solicitor by the name of Hawkins. He has found for me an estate in London and the legalities should be finalized within the next few months. As such, I make preparations for the voyage. My brides will remain here in Transylvania. I have informed Lavinia that she will be in charge and to await word that I have need of them.

From the journal of Vlad Dracula
1890

My solicitor, Hawkins has taken ill and has thus sent his young associate, a man by the name of Harker, to tend to the legalities of my relocation. I have persuaded him to aid me in my English pronunciations. These lessons are proceeding nicely, though each night the man becomes more certain that something is amiss.

I do not wish to dispose of Harker so near to my journey, but may be forced to do so. Already, he has attempted to send unauthorized correspondences to his homeland through the Szygany and I fear he may become truly troublesome.

From the journal of Vlad Dracula
1890

I arrived in England by ship.

Never before have I allowed myself to be at the mercy of others, and this to such an extent. For during the daylight hours I was confined, a prisoner within a large wooden crate which served as a casket. Seamen as a whole are a superstitious breed and several times I overheard them arguing, some wanting to throw "the accursed crate" into the sea, others desiring to set it ablaze.

The captain, a man with a mind toward profit, refused, stating that he had taken responsibility for his client's goods and that it was his duty to deliver these as promised. He was able to keep the men at bay for the early part of the journey, but I had need to feed and so, each morning that another sailor went missing, apprehension grew. Still, the captain stayed true to his word.

In the end, he died as readily as did his crew.

I shipped with me several large containers of earth from my homeland. Though, contrary to much speculation by those that hunt my kind, these are not critical to my survival. The soil of a nosferatu's native land does contain certain energizing and curative agents and we are weakened in its absence. As I choose to live at length in a new land, I felt it best to bring with me as much of this regenerating earth as I deemed practical. My body needs time to acclimate to the new environ and I am somewhat weakened and more easily slain when not anchored to native soil.

From the journal of Vlad Dracula
1890

I have selected my first bride in this new land. Her name Is Lucy Westenra and she is young and vibrant, a woman of means and trained in the ways and courtesies of the social elite. I have chosen to proceed slowly, drinking regularly from her and then offering my own veins for her, but stopping short of causing death.

My hope is that this gradual process may create a more complete bond between us, that in this way, perhaps I can finally find someone with whom I can truly unite, someone capable of sharing my sorrows through the eternal midnight. She is not as fiery as Lavinia and lacks Sevda's intellect. In truth, I feel that her social status combined with her irrefutable beauty has left her somewhat superficial. But this will change as she transforms into something she cannot yet imagine. I look forward to the time when we feed together as one and then walk the lanes as a sophisticated couple, attending the theatre, socializing with pompous politicians and brilliant artists, enjoying all that this great city has to offer. Such a time that will be.

From the journal of Vlad Dracula
1890

I have underestimated Lucy's value to those about her. Not only has her betrothed personally set about to thwart my efforts, but others have assembled by her side. One of these, a Dutchman by the name of Van Helsing, has considerable knowledge concerning the nosferatu and recognizes her illness for what it is. He is a clever and devious foe, learned and open to concepts that other modern men shun as nonsense. I must consider each action carefully, for a truly dangerous opponent has learned of my true nature and makes plans to eliminate me. I am no longer free to move about at will and must make plans to ensure my survival.

[Note: It pleases me greatly to report that this is the final entry in the journal of Vlad Dracula – Abraham Van Helsing]

From the journal of Charles Van Helsing
February 13, 1930

Oh, the things in my head. The haunted thoughts. The anger, the hate.

Pop is dead. He's dead! And nothing can change that. But, the things I could do.

The things I will do.

Oh, I know what you're thinking. I'm just a bookkeeper. I'd be lucky if I even knew how to fire a weapon. Our entire bootlegging organization is insignificant. Our one and only raid wasn't even manned by our employees, but by Johnny's schoolmates. I'm incapable of revenge.

Why, yes. I suppose I am.

But there is another who is far greater than Capone or any number of his men.

Oh, I admit it. I'm appalled by my own plan. I rail at myself and curse my own name. What fool, what bloodthirsty fool would conceive such a thing?

But here's the thing. Shh, shh, here's the secret. Can you keep it?

The idea's not mine.

No, really. I'm sure of it.

This thought was given to me by another, pressed into my mind in the hours of despair following my father's murder. My intellect recognizes it for what it is, the manipulations of a monster.

Strange how that knowledge doesn't concern me.

Perhaps you think I've gone crazy.

Well, if so, it's not entirely unpleasant. How very peculiar. I think I now may understand the motivations of the mental patient Renfield as described by Dr. Seward in his journal.

Well, sanity aside, I should probably record the events as they occurred. Just on the off chance that there would be some need.

Just allow me a moment to put my thoughts in order. That's not all that easy it seems, so forgive my detours and asides.

Now, let's see. Yes. In the hours following Pop's death I secluded myself in my room. Mom, Johnny, even Mavis attempted to coax me out, but I had no desire to speak to anyone. I was furious at Johnny. Murderously mad. This was his fault. His! But I couldn't say this publically. No, no, no. Mom couldn't be allowed to know of Johnny's guilt. There's no need for her to carry the burden of that knowledge.

And what about the knowledge of my involvement? Better we forget that, don't you think?

Oh, it was a high price.

Much too high.

But Pop's death seems to have shocked Johnny out of his gangster fantasy. His hero, his idol, Capone, was responsible for our father's death. I can assure you, Johnny will never again emulate him. Gone are the pinstriped suits, the fedoras, and brash attitude. Gone is the cocky strut. He's even trying to change his speech patterns. Well, good riddance. I lost my father to his adolescent nonsense. The least he can do is suffer.

That sounds bitter, doesn't it?

Well, its anger only, not hatred.

And so I locked myself away where I wouldn't be tempted to blurt the truth, to ruin relationships and damage this already grieving woman whom I love so dearly.

Evening turned into midnight and still I sat there alone. Just me and my thoughts.

And those other thoughts.

I found myself drawn to the journal of Dracula. Not to the English translation, but to the original tome.

I lifted the precious volume, running my fingers across the leather. It was coarse to the touch but worn smooth in many areas through handling. For several moments I simply stared at the cover. Maybe I realized that I was about to cross into something beyond my comprehension, that if I opened this book there would be no turning back.

Oh, but hadn't I already traveled that path?

I'd held this same book numerous times. I'd flipped through the pages. For crying out loud, I'd scraped blood from the leaves and consumed it! Why was I afraid now?

Because this was different.

I knew it was different.

If there'd been any question that another intelligence was directing my actions, well, that question was answered. For, when I opened the book, miraculously, I found that I could read the document.

It wasn't English, probably some precursor to what became Romanian.

I hadn't studied it.

I don't have any background in linguistics. But yet I could read it as well as I could read my own writing. Sure, I could have questioned how this could be, but I already knew.

I had partaken of Dracula's blood.

Flipping through the yellowed pages, my trembling hands directed as if from some outside force, I discovered a passage my great uncle – that rascally fox – had omitted from his translation.

The passage that details how Dracula may be revived.

I felt nauseous at this find.

Absolutely elated!

For the implications were so very clear even to my clouded grief-stricken mind.

I sat there. Simply staring at the yellowed pages, at the precise aggressive script, at the words themselves. And I knew what was to come. I could see it all as if watching it happen before my own eyes.

Let me be clear.

I've heard no words from Dracula. He hasn't spoken to me in any tangible way, he hasn't come calling or whispered in my ear. But still I know that he's made a pact with me. If I revive him, if I bring him forth from the grave, he will avenge my father's death. And Lord in heaven, to the damnation of my very soul, I plan to do it.

From the journal of Charles Van Helsing
February 20, 1930

I don't want to write. I don't! In fact, I almost burned this damn journal. This evidence! Almost. But I guess am holding on to just enough of myself to recognize its potential value.

What value!

To whom?

No.

Stop.

Breathe.

I will do this.

I will record these events even if I no longer understand why.

But, well, I do hate to leave a record of actions that will be illegal and unethical. Not wise, I suppose. But, well, yes, you've convinced me. I'll continue. Just understand, this is more difficult than you know.

But, enough already. On with it.

I've never flown in an airplane before.

The experience was terrifying. The metal monstrosity pitched and dove seemingly with every gust. The propellers whined in constant complaint. The wings flexed and wobbled. I sat rigid, clasping the arm rests while other travelers laughed and boasted of their country clubs or African safaris, of their acquisitions and mergers.

They stared at me. Laughed. Am I some sideshow freak?

Air travel is for the ultra-rich and this does not include me. I'm sure that's why they stared. Only that.

I was only able to afford such a trip by a very strange circumstance.

You've guessed it, haven't you?

I had help.

Yes, just as I'd felt directed to read the formerly unreadable pages of Dracula's journal, I was also guided to inspect another old tome. And hidden within the pages, I discovered several substantial bank notes. Plenty enough for a round trip to Amsterdam and for my needs once I arrived.

Such a clever monster.

Had Dracula, though dead for decades, somehow directed those funds to be put there for the purpose of aiding in his resurrection?

Of course he had. But, who had he controlled? Had it been my great uncle? Or maybe someone closer. Maybe Hans. I'm thinking Hans. Though wouldn't it be ironic if he'd subjected my Uncle Abraham to his will? His nemesis. Oh, that would be delightful!

From the journal of Charles Van Helsing
February 22, 1930

As you may have suspected from recent entries, I'm finding it difficult to collect coherent thoughts. But still, I feel the need to record these events as I remember them. I'm truly not myself and wonder if I ever will be again. But the madness seems to come in waves, allowing me the opportunity to function, to be about my heinous task, and even to scribble these few words.

But that doesn't matter to you, does it?

You're curious. Everyone's curious. Well, so am I. And what insight I have is no insight at all. Foolishness! You're all filled with foolishness!

I'm sorry. That was, well, like I said, difficulty with coherent thoughts.

I'll put the pen down for a couple of minutes while I try to push my brain back into my head.

Alright. Better now.

I think I can proceed, but I'd better get to it. No telling what kind of random impulses will lash out if I don't stay on task.

The family crypt is located in a small private cemetery about an hour outside of Amsterdam. After some maneuvering and a bit of bribery I was able to rent a car as I didn't want to take a taxi cab and risk the driver witnessing my grave robbery. I suppose that means I've retained at least some little common sense.

The area is rural and the roads poorly maintained. I was lucky to make the journey without a broken axle.

It was evening when finally I made my way to the grounds. This was timed purposely as I wanted to avoid contact with others.

My precautions proved unnecessary, as I soon became convinced that no one, not even a groundskeeper, had entered in several years. The heavy iron gate was rusted and hanging at a slight angle. It took some effort to force it open, but when finally it moved, it did so with a groaning creak that could probably be heard for the better part of a mile. Though it was winter, still I could see that the grounds were overgrown. Vines wrapped about tombstones, weeds covered the frozen ground. No flowers adorned a grave.

I saw the remains of several small creatures: cats, dogs, rabbits. Some of the carcasses seemed relatively recent while others were nothing but bones. All of the more recent specimens had slashed necks. I have a feeling the others, had there still been flesh, would have displayed similar wounds. I should have run very fast and very far. And if I'd been in full control of myself this is exactly what I would have done.

But there's the other.

The one that has managed to squirrel into my brain.

Does it trouble you that I've no true desire to fight against the influence?

Oh, I recognize the danger. I suspect the consequences. But then I think of my father lying dead in the street, gunned down by Capone's thugs. I think of Johnny stumbling into our kitchen, Pop's blood on his shirt and hands, screaming with grief as he somehow managed to relate the tragedy. I think of my mother crumbling to the floor in fits of hysterics, nearly dying when she heard the horrible news. And I set aside my concerns and allow the other, that non-voice, to guide me toward an eventual revenge. Sweet, precious revenge.

And so there I was, in the graveyard.

The door to the crypt was ajar.

How convenient.

It's almost as if the way had been prepared for me.

Despite my weakness, I paused before the door. I guess you could say this was my final battle against the fiend that guided my steps. Twice, I stepped away, determined to return to the car and to flee this city – this continent – before I could do something that could never be undone. I circled the crypt, just looking at it, fighting my conflicting urges, talking myself both in and then out of each decision, simultaneously terrified and yet exhilarated. But finally I paused, stared at the cold gray stone, told myself that it wouldn't hurt just to look inside. I wouldn't remove anything from the tomb. I wouldn't go through with this insane plan. Of course I wouldn't. I'd just have a peek. After all, I'd come all this way.

Yes. Even in my compromised state I recognize this as rationalization. But it's how I gained the courage to do the deed. One tiny self-deception followed by another and then another. I am a bundle of contradictions, aren't I?

They appeared just before I entered the crypt. Three large birds, dark in color, perched in a row along the fence top. I could swear they were staring at me, following me with their soulless eyes.

Of course they were.

Black eyes, red at the core, deep rich crimson, nearly iridescent.

No matter how hard I tried to turn away, my eyes were drawn to them. There was something wrong about these things, something horrible, something I should recognize. But my cloudy mind couldn't connect my thoughts. But even so, something within me told me that these birds weren't right. Some last scrap of sanity told me to flee these things.

Breaking their gaze, I hurried into the crypt, leaving the door open as I stepped down into the darkened space. Glancing back, I half expected the birds to have followed me, but they were nowhere to be seen. Thank God! Because I'm sure I would have lost all strength and sense had they followed.

There was a torch mounted on the wall and I lit it with a wooden match I'd carried in my pocket for this specific purpose.

There were five caskets in this tomb. Abraham's was alone against the far wall. Strange marks, they almost seemed to be symbols, were scratched into the wood, claw marks, but almost, it seemed, with intent. But no. This had to be the result of an animal. A large dog? Maybe even a bear.

Did it matter?

Anything!

Did anything matter? Why should I care about beasts carving symbols into a casket?

I stared at the damaged coffin, just staring, not really focusing. I think by this point I knew that any rationality was lost, that my course was set. Eventually I reached out, placing both hands at the rim of the lid.

The casket wasn't sealed and I was able to lift the top with little difficulty. I guess you could call this another mystery. Why was the lid left unsecured? But honestly, by this point I'd given up on asking about these small twists of unlikely luck. By whatever means, everything was set in place, the chest delivered by my uncle, the journal calling to me, the preparations for my arrival. It had all been planned. And now this. Grave robbery. To think, a year ago I was at Yale. What would people think?

My great uncle lay there, his arms at his sides, eyes and lips closed. The skin was dark and pulled tightly against the bones, a handful of white tufts still clung to the top of his skull, the teeth were yellow and exposed. My one reprieve was that the odor was mild. I don't know if this is common for a cadaver of this age or if some other factors were in motion, but I was thankful nonetheless.

The urn was there, shoved into a corner beside Abraham's right foot. Simple unadorned ceramic. So plain. So apparently harmless. So deceptive.

I reached in. My fingers found and then clutched the cold hard ceramic.

I moved away quickly, fearful that I'd lose my nerve.

As I stepped from the tomb, the urn cradled in the crook of my right arm, I found that I was not alone.

They were there.

The three of them.

I knew who they were immediately.

The brides of Dracula.

Each wore a white lace gown, but the clothing was tattered and yellowed, spotted with filth and blood. Their eyes were wild, their movements catlike. They cocked their heads, shifting forward and back, glancing at one another and then at me. The thought came to me that this was more like crossing a wolf pack than a group of women. Obviously these three had not fared well in the four decades since their master's death.

And yet, somehow they'd found this place.

Somehow they'd traveled from Transylvania to Amsterdam. Dracula had called them. I'm sure of it. For whatever reason these vampires weren't capable of resurrecting him themselves, but still he'd called them to his gravesite to guard his remains. And so they had, decade after decade, remaining here, likely feeding off of animals and the occasional person, losing what little humanity they had possessed to the passing years.

They encircled me. Each crouched as if poised to spring, each sniffing the air. Hissing. Cooing. One by one they bore their teeth. How can I describe this? Their canines were extended and obviously sharp, very very sharp. They were whiter than any natural teeth I'd ever seen. Their design seemed more like a shark's tooth I'd once seen at the Field Museum than that of a human or any other mammal. It seemed they were rather flat and wide at the gum and curved down to a very narrow point. They were long but not freakishly so, perhaps twice the length of normal canines. I could see how these monsters could hide them easily enough by not opening the mouth too wide.

I had no idea what they intended to do. Would they steal my blood to spill over Dracula's ashes? Did they know some means of reviving him that hadn't been revealed to me in the journals? But if so, why wait so long? Why wait for me to come? Wouldn't anyone do?

One of the vampires, a dark haired beast that seemed to be the leader of the pack, moved closer, sniffing me and giggling almost like a young child. My guess is that this was Lavinia, Dracula's first bride. He had described her as beautiful, and I'm sure that she once was – there was still some small hint of this – but now she is a beast only, all higher reasoning having fled long ago. She circled me, her face less than an inch away, sniffing, sniffing. She slid her fingers across my chest and snorted like a disinterested dog.

Another approached and then another, each touching me, running claw-like fingers across my form. One licked my neck. Another giggled. I wanted so much to run, but it was as if an invisible hand held me to my place.

Strangely, and this didn't occur to me till much later, none sought to touch the urn.

There came a point that they all pulled away nearly as one. Each had touched me, sniffed at me, licked me, and violated me by rubbing against me as if in lust. And then they were gone. Just gone. As if they'd never existed.

Can I tell you just how horrified I am?

Letter from Johnny Van Helsing to Hans Van Helsing
February 26, 1930

Hans,

Charlie came back today. He was gone almost a week. He just left. Didn't say where he was going or even that he was going. No note or anything. So nice of him.

Then he came back, barely said a word, just went into his room and locked the door. So I started pounding and yelling at him, "Hey, Charlie! Open up. We've got to talk." He didn't come out until after midnight.

I tried to talk to him then, you know, to tell him about Ma, how she'd gotten worse while he was gone, how I really thought we were going to lose her, that his disappearing could have been the final thing that did her in. But it was like he didn't hear. He just walked past me with this plain-looking ceramic pot in one hand and that old book in the other and went to the basement door. The sap locked it behind him. He was down there the rest of the night. Not a word from him. I'm really worried about him, Hans, and don't know what to do. I really wish you'd come for a visit.

Johnny

From the journal of Charles Van Helsing
February 26, 1930

Johnny came pounding on my bedroom door this morning until finally, despite my clouded head, I had to let him in before he upset Mom. He was furious of course. I hadn't told him where I'd been or why, and I'm not sure that I ever will. And what right does he have to my private affairs anyway?

But there's something else. Something... My mind's so cluttered, I can't think of what's... It's almost like...

Well, I'm not sure what I was going to say there. I lost the thought. I think maybe I was...

Maybe it would be better if I finished this entry later.

From the journal of Charles Van Helsing
February 26, 1930

I think I'm better now. At least in terms of focus. I'm not sure how long my mind will be my own, so allow me to continue where I left off.

Johnny came to my room and asked where I'd been. He told me that Mom had become worse, that she wouldn't even listen to her radio dramas or work on her crosswords. Johnny's tough guy gangster façade is gone and it was good to see my true brother again, not the tough kid trying to imitate a gangster, just a frightened seventeen year-old whose world was crumbling around him. Good to see the change, bad to know the circumstances that created it.

And though I was happy to see the new Johnny, I was less than thrilled at his accusations. "All you do is hide in this room. You don't know how Ma is. You don't know what it's like to try to run the business by myself. You just disappear for six days and don't tell me anything."

Straining to remain focused, I said, "Things are strange right now. I don't want you hurt."

"Yeah, yeah, big brother doesn't want to hurt me. What do you think you're doing with all your secrets? Do you think it helps me when you disappear and I've got to take care of Ma and the business? You think she doesn't know you were gone? What was I supposed to say to her?"

What could I say? He was right. I said nothing.

Johnny shook his head, disgusted at me. "You don't even care, do you?"

I reached out, touching him at the shoulder. He shrugged me off. "Don't touch me. You ain't got the right anymore."

"Johnny. Listen. I do care."

"If you care so much then why weren't you here helping me?" This was nearly a yell, but I could tell he was trying to keep his volume under control for fear of upsetting Mom in the next room over.

I met his gaze. "I have something going on. When it's over, you'll understand. Just be patient."

"Patient? You're twenty-two. I'm only seventeen. Aren't you the one who's supposed to be patient with me?" I nearly smiled. It wasn't often Johnny admitted that he needed help from his older brother.

"We both know Pop wanted you to take charge of the business when he was gone."

"I don't think he was planning on being gone so soon," shot Johnny.

And then we became silent. We both knew why Pop had been gunned down. Johnny had to be wondering if I was going to take this opportunity to remind him of his blame. I was wondering the same thing. "It wasn't your fault," I said after several moments. "Things just got out of control."

"Liar."

I shrugged.

"When you disappeared," he said, his voice nearly cracking. "I was worried, you know, that it was the same thing that happened to Pa."

This struck me like a blow from Jack Dempsey. I hadn't thought of this, that after Pop, Johnny and Mom might assume something similar had happened to me. "My God, Johnny. I never thought about that."

"What? That your family might worry? Yeah, why would you think something like that?"

We found silence again. It was our only refuge.

Johnny stared at his hands. He was twirling my father's ring around one of his fingers. It was a poor fit. "A girl came looking for you," he said in an abrupt change of subject.

"What? Who?"

"Some girl named Pearl. Colored. She said she knows you from some book store. Said she saw you a while back staring through the window, but you ran away when she saw you. She said you looked panicked and kind of crazy. I guess she was worried when you never showed up again."

"Did she say anything about why I was there?"

Johnny shrugged. "Nah. I can guess though. Vampires, right?"

I decided not to answer the question. "How did she know where to look for me?"

"She knew your name. Our laundromats are named Van Helsing. She put two and two, showed up at one of the shops. I just happened to be there when she came in."

I nodded.

"She's nice, you know. Real nice. Pretty too. That doesn't hurt either."

"Don't get any ideas."

"Why? You're engaged."

"You know as well as I do that I have no intention of marrying Mavis."

Johnny shrugged and grinned. "What do you think Ma would say if you brought home a colored girl?"

"Not her concern. Just, Johnny. I think I might like this girl, but the timing's poor."

Johnny grinned. "Eh, you know me."

"Yes I do. Don't get any ideas."

We both chuckled. It felt good.

After another moment, Johnny turned serious again. "What was going on last night?"

"What do you mean?"

"You know what I mean. Last night, you went into the basement and locked me out. You wouldn't even look at me when I talked to you."

And here my stomach took a twist. I had absolutely no memory of this encounter or of what I'd done in the basement.

From the journal of Charles Van Helsing
March 3, 1930

I'm not Charlie. This is me, Johnny. I'm writing in here because these things need to be put down someplace and Charlie, well let's just say he wasn't really present at the time. I just read this journal so now I know what's been going on with him, why he's been acting so bonkers. What I'm writing here has to do with that.

I don't really know where to begin. It was late, maybe two in the morning when I heard a commotion from the basement. This horrible scream and something like a rushing wind. I got up as fast as I could and went to the door, but it was locked. Charlie always keeps things locked these days.

There's a key. I guess I could've used it any time before, but even though he was making me as mad as a hornet I wanted to give him privacy. But this was different. Something was really wrong down there.

By the time I got the door open, the wind sounds were gone and the howls had turned to these low growling moans. I wondered what exactly it was that Charlie's been doing down here. And I wished I'd brought a gun or at least a baseball bat or something because this place just didn't feel right.

When I was halfway down the stairs I saw Charlie lying on the floor all curled up. He wasn't moving and I was wondering if he was even breathing. I took another couple of steps before I realized he wasn't alone down there.

I know this will sound nuts, but you're reading this journal. You already know everything's nuts.

There was a vampire down there with him. I know you'll want to know how I could tell what it was, but just trust me.

The vampire was naked. And pale. Like the color of milk, or like he'd never seen the sun ever, which, I guess makes sense considering. His face was bony like there was barely a layer of skin over the skull. The rest of his body too, real skinny, real pale. His white hair was long and sticking out all over like it'd never been combed. And his teeth. He had the teeth. You know, the vampire teeth. Long and sharp. Razor sharp by the look of them.

My first thought was to run away, to lock the door behind me and just get out of there. But Charlie was down there and I didn't know if he was dead or alive. And so I just stood there like a goof, just looking at this thing.

And then I realized it was him that I'd heard moaning. The vampire. And the thing didn't even seem to know I was there. He was just sitting there on the floor, maybe ten feet away from Charlie. There was a bunch of broken pieces of something around him, the urn, I'm guessing. And he was holding that old book, the one Charlie keeps obsessing over. The vampire was staring at the book and some-times sniffing at it like a dog. He wasn't reading it or anything. It wasn't even open. He was just, I don't know, mesmerized, just gazing at the thing all glassy eyed.

I took a step, just testing. I wanted to see if he'd look at me. I must be crazy as my brother because there's no sane reason to go down there like that. But I did it. My hands were shaking and my legs were wanting to run the other way. But the vampire didn't seem to notice me. He was just staring at that book. Like I say, sniffing at it, rubbing it real gentle like. It was the strangest thing I ever seen.

I took another step.

And then another.

There was a weird smell in the basement. Almost like meat gone bad, but there was something more to it than that. Whatever it was, it made me feel like I was going to vomit.

I took a couple more steps, and a couple more.

God, I was scared, all the time telling myself I was bonkers for going down there. All the time just wanting to run upstairs, pull Ma out of bed, and leave this crazy place.

And maybe I would have, but I swear the vampire didn't even know I was there. He was just blotto.

But now what? I needed to get Charlie out of there, but how was I supposed to carry him up those stairs? And would the vampire let me? I mean, he was ignoring me now, but if I tried to take Charlie, that would be pretty obvious.

I glanced over at Charlie. He still hadn't moved. The vampire was still ob-sessed with his book. In fact, by this time he had the corner of it in his mouth, gnawing on it like a dog with a bone.

I was stuck. I couldn't figure that the vampire would just sit there forever. I mean, he has to feed, right? But I couldn't leave Charlie just lying there. I'd already lost Pa, I'd be damned if I was going to lose my brother. So I started looking around the basement, just trying to see if there was anything that could help me somehow. I really didn't even know what I was looking for. A weapon, I guess.

I thought about maybe getting a shovel of hot coals from the furnace and throwing them at him, but guessed that would just get him mad. Whatever trance he was in, I had a feeling it would break if I tried to hurt him. And I don't know how to kill a vampire. I mean, I've heard some things, me and Charlie saw that movie, Nosferatu, I read some stories in the pulps, but I really don't know anything real. I mean, kill a monster with a garlic clove or a cross? Are they serious?

But there's Charlie, still on the floor, not moving. Maybe dead, maybe not. So I took a step, just a little one, testing the boundaries. The vampire just kept sucking on the corner of his book like a baby with a pacifier. The only problem was this baby had teeth to make the big bad wolf jealous.

And then I saw it, the chain and collar we used when we had our mastiff. The dog's name was Moses and he was huge, like a hundred-sixty pounds huge. The chain was staked into the wall and the collar was still attached to the chain. A big thick chain. And I got the craziest idea in my head. And it had to be crazy, because there was no way that vampire was going to let me just walk up to him and slip a collar over his head.

But that was my brilliant plan. Chain the vampire to the wall with the dog chain. I guess they call Charlie the smart one for a reason.

So, I crept around the room, staying tight against the wall, all the while watching the vampire as he cradled his book. By this time he'd taken to licking it and then rubbing it against his face. Lick, rub, lick, rub. It seemed maybe he was barely aware of anything around him.

I can't tell you how scared I was when I picked up that chain. In fact, I dropped it pretty much right away. My hands were just jittering so bad. The vampire stopped what he was doing and stared around, cocking his head like he was listening for something. I was sure I was dead. I knew he would turn around and take a big chomp out of my neck with those big nasty teeth.

But instead, he just went back to staring at his book.

After a couple of minutes of trying not to wet myself, I took a step forward. What was I thinking? This was a truly unintelligent idea. But Charlie. I couldn't just leave him there. I mean, if Charlie wasn't already dead, well that vampire was going to get hungry eventually, right?

So, I moved up behind the vampire. I had the collar opened wide. The plan was to slip it around his neck, fasten it, and then get as far away as I could as fast as I could. I mean, I didn't expect that collar to hold him long. All he had to do was unfasten the thing. It wasn't like there was a lock on it or anything.

The thing of it is, it worked. Pretty much exactly as I planned. I learned later that the vampire had just been revived after being dead for a few decades. He hadn't come back into his senses yet and so, yeah, I was able to slip the collar on, fasten it, and then get Charlie out. All the while the vampire just sat there staring at that stupid book.

As to Charlie, well, he's alive. I guess that's a start.

From the journal of Charles Van Helsing
March 5, 1930

I'm my own man again. Or, maybe I should say, I hope I'm my own man. If Dracula's influence remains, it's diminished. My guess is that whatever thing had taken up residence in my brain went back to him when he regained his physical body.

The other theory is that the vampire's control will return as he regains his mind. For right now he's as he'd described himself when first he'd risen as nosferatu: mindless, beast-like, devoid of memory or language. I can only assume that, as in his first rebirth, his mental facilities will return. By that point, we'd better have a plan.

As to the resurrection of Dracula, I'll give only a few details. Like my great uncle, I feel those specifics are best kept a mystery. Don't come to me for how-to instructions on vampire resurrection. You won't get that here. But I do feel it's important to commit the event to paper before something happens to silence me forever. And yes, I do have a sense that this will somehow be my end. I can't say why. Maybe it's just fear, maybe I'm just obsessing over my own mortality, but I did resurrect a vampire. There's risk involved.

So, as to Dracula. The process took several days and honestly I remember very little of it. Each night I would leave my room and lock myself into the basement. I did this as if in a trance, little or no self-will.

There was a ritual involved. Some strange passages read from the journal, probably in a language that predates Christ. As with so many things these days, I have no idea of how I came to read these words.

The resurrection happened on the fourth or fifth day after my return. As on previous days I chanted the ancient spell and added certain substances to Dracula's ashes, the most significant being several drops of my own blood which I obtained by pricking my finger. After this, I would scrape some of his blood from the journal pages into the mixture and then repeat the strange and melodic words.

The resurrection affected me physically. My entire form broke into shivers. I began sweating profusely. It felt as if my insides were wrenched from my body.

The urn, situated on a small end table, bobbled and danced and then fell breaking on the hard concrete floor. The ashes splashed out across the floor and, writhing in pain, I fell to beside them. All I knew was pain. And then darkness. Real darkness, the midnight black of hell and the grave. I remember nothing else, but Johnny has already recounted what happened next.

From the journal of Charles Van Helsing
March 10, 1930

On the first day following Dracula's resurrection Johnny bought some heavier chains and locks which he cemented into the floor. After the cement set for a day or so he secured Dracula by neck, hand, and foot. This was all before the vampire came out of his initial stupor which lasted for about three days. After that, Dracula began howling and loping back and forth, tugging on his restraints, and growling whenever we'd enter. The dog collar and chain would have never held.

Mom has questioned the noise coming from the basement. Johnny told her that he's keeping a dog for a sick friend, but I don't think she believes it. Thankfully, she's been kind enough to pretend to accept the lie. She's so frail. Her color is poor, she has no appetite, and trembles even when the temperature is warm. Most days are spent staring through the window and listening to radio dramas like Amos and Andy. But she stares at me now, this strange expression on her face. I don't know what she's thinking, but won't ask her because of the questions she may ask.

I guess I should say something about Johnny.

He's changed. Drastically. I can't tell you how proud I am of my little brother. He's been running the business, both sides of it. Sure, he makes some mistakes, but overall he's a competent manager. Now that I'm more myself again, I step in while he's in school to keep things moving, but he's the real brain behind the operation. He's always seemed to have unrealized potential. I'm sure you know the type. He was one of those boys with too much energy and too much curiosity. The type that always wants to explore something new or get into something that shouldn't be gotten into. The kind that make parents want to rip out their hair. But it seems to me that this is the type of person that, as an adult, might be capable of great things. That drive and curiosity has the capacity to take them to places that most of us would never imagine.

The only thing that still concerned me about Johnny was his reluctance to participate in my plan of revenge.

"You're bonkers," he said when I presented the plan. "You came up with this when that thing was controlling you."

"Yes," I said. "The idea came from the demon. That doesn't make it a bad plan."

Johnny looked as if he might deck me. "You're dumber than a toad, I hope you know that. He just gave you that stupid idea so you'd revive him."

"Of course he did. And I followed through with my part of the bargain. Now it's time for him to fulfil his."

Johnny rolled his eyes as if looking for divine confirmation that his brother had slipped into permanent insanity. "You really think you can control him? You really think he'll hold up his end? 'Cause I got me a real strong idea he won't."

I stared at him directly, keeping my voice even yet firm. I wanted this to sink in. "I'm trying to avenge our father's death because the person responsible for it doesn't seem to want to bother."

I might as well have slapped him in the face. He went pale. His mouth opened and then closed silently. I didn't give him a chance to formulate a response.

"Pop's dead because of your shortsighted plan. Now, I'm trying to clean up after you. Will you at least have the decency to help me?"

"That's not fair."

"What's not fair is what happened to Pop. What's not fair is what it's doing to Mom."

"You're a bastard, you know that?"

"Maybe. But you're going to help me with this because if you don't and something happens to me or Mom you'll never forgive yourself."

I left him there to contemplate his situation.

Apparently, I can be a real snake when the need arises.

From the journal of Charles Van Helsing
March 12, 1930

Johnny's still not happy about my plan, but is my reluctant partner like I was for him when we hijacked Capone's delivery. I suppose fair is fair. But I don't really care what Johnny thinks. I love him deeply but I must admit, I'll probably never forgive him. I can't imagine life without him and sometimes I have the urge to give the boy a hug and tell him how much he means to me, that he's got that special spark, that fiery charisma, that I would be lost without him, but underneath I know I'd still have a father if not for Johnny. And that's a hard thing to get past.

But, I suppose you'd rather hear about the vampire.

Dracula's feedings are about as disgusting as anything I've ever seen. We've been shooting rats with B. B. guns and feeding them to Dracula. He takes the rats, some dead, but mostly the wounded ones, sinks his long razor-like teeth into them and sucks them dry of blood before crushing them in his hands. He seems to take pleasure in these revolting acts because he grins and chuckles and sometimes even slaps his palms on the concrete in delight. More often than not, he hurls the bloodless carcasses at us and then chuckles at our revulsion. We've still not determined how we're going to get this beast to follow our plan and all logic tells me we've stepped into something more horrible than I could have ever imagined.

From the journal of Charles Van Helsing
March 14, 1930

I'll try to recount everything as it happened tonight, but it was chaotic and unsettling.

Johnny and I descended the stairs to feed Dracula. The vampire was fully alert and the single bare lightbulb caused his bone white skin to gleam like a beacon in the semidarkness. He'd been crawling around the floor, sniffing at the concrete like a hound following a scent. He was still naked because it was simply too risky to dress him. His white hair hung in clumps. He drooled and spat, shifted from side to side, and nibbled at his own hands causing them to bleed. When we entered, he stopped what he was doing and stared at us, his dark eyes narrow, his lips curled back, teeth bared.

I leaned near to Johnny and whispered, "He seems more intense tonight."

Johnny shrugged, probably trying to cover his own unease. "He still doesn't seem too smart or too human."

"You've read his journals. You know what he is."

Johnny looked at me. "I know what he used to be. But he died and disintegrated to dust forty years ago. How do we know if he'll ever get his mind back? Maybe he'll just stay like this."

Johnny had a good point. Was it possible that Dracula would never regain his intellect? Was it possible that we could use him for our revenge and then kill him again before he ever became crafty and clever? Wouldn't that be best for all? Because the last thing we wanted was for Dracula to remember all of his extraordinary abilities. There'd be no way to contain him if he could shapeshift into a smaller creature or transform into a mist. We'd be entirely at his mercy.

It was Johnny's turn to feed the beast and so he held up the burlap sack containing the rats, allowing Dracula to see that there was movement from within. The vampire motioned with his hands, indicating in crud uncoordinated gestures for us to bring it closer. The monster was hungry.

As was our habit, Johnny tossed the bag toward the vampire. But it fell a couple of feet short of Dracula's reach, hitting the floor with a shuffling thump. The few living rats squealed and kicked from within.

The vampire hissed with frustration as he stretched his chains in an attempt to reach the squirming sack. Johnny took a step forward, planning to kick the sack to within Dracula's reach.

"Careful. Don't get too close," I warned.

"I'm okay," said Johnny, but I could tell he was nervous. He hadn't been this close to the vampire since the first days when Dracula had been docile and in a near stupor.

Johnny kicked the sack. It moved, but not far enough.

He kicked it again. This time it began to roll but had little momentum and unbalanced weight distribution. It settled back into about the same spot. Dracula was growling and reaching forward, a white lather bubbling at his lips.

Johnny leaned forward, apparently deciding to pick up the sack and heave it toward Dracula instead of inching it forward with his foot. But as he clutched the bag, his head and shoulders moved forward, closer to Dracula than the sack he was lifting.

The vampire's lunge was faster than I could have imagined. Dracula grabbed Johnny by the collar and pulled him close as my brother screamed and cursed.

I snatched the shovel that leaned against the wall by the furnace and raced forward, striking Dracula several times with the pointed iron head of the thing.

Still the vampire clung to Johnny who was beating at him frantically with his fists and kicking wildly.

I jabbed and hit and even tried to wedge the shovel between the two. In a desperate effort, I reared back and swung the shovel as hard as I could, connecting with Dracula at the top of his head.

The vampire was momentarily distracted and released his grip.

Johnny scrambled free of his clutches as Dracula regained his bearings, turned sharply left, and grabbed me with both hands, pulling me to him, pressing my face against his bare chest. I could feel him sniffing at me and running his fingers over my neck. Here it was. I was about to die.

With a harsh jerk to my shoulders, Dracula pulled me upward and back so that he could stare at my face. Our gazes met and for several seconds we studied one another. I'm not sure what he saw of me, likely a terrified young man and nothing more, but I stared into a most peculiar face, a frightening face, the face of both a monster and a man. The eyes were large and dark, the nose prominent and bonelike, the cheeks high and narrow. His lips were full, his forehead broad. His hair was a tangled white bird nest nearly matching his complexion.

With only the whisper of a grin, Dracula touched two fingers to his lips, holding these in this manner for several seconds as if in a prolonged kiss, before then placing these fingers upon my lips in like manner. He repeated this three times and then grunted approval, nodded, and then released me.

He released me!

I was too shocked, too confused to flee, and so continued to stare at him. Had he recognized something in me, perhaps some remnant of his former control? Had he just placed some new curse on me? I felt no different. I could sense no intrusion. What had just occurred?

Finally, Johnny's yelling pierced my mind and the trance was broken. I scrambled away from Dracula, not looking back until I was near the staircase.

My senses now engaged, my thoughts returned to my brother. "Are you bitten?" I screamed. "Are you bitten?"

Johnny had fallen to his knees, his palms on the concrete floor. He was vomiting, whether from shock and fear or from something more sinister, I couldn't tell.

"Are you bitten?" I screamed again.

Johnny shook his head. "No," he gasped, wiping spittle from his lips with the back of a hand. "No. I don't think so."

Relieved, I sank to the floor beside him, exhausted and confused, my mind racing with questions. After a few moments I caught Dracula's gaze. He was kneeling, palms pressed against his chest as if in some ritualistic posture, studying us intently, his gaze unwavering.

Letter from Johnny Van Helsing to Hans Van Helsing
March 17, 1930

Uncle Hans,

This is probably the strangest letter I've ever written. And I'll tell you right now, it's all true, not a fib or a tall tale in the whole thing. I've told you a lot about Charlie lately, about how he believes all of the vampire stuff from those books and pages you gave him. Well what I haven't told you on account of I just didn't know how to say it without sounding bonkers is that it's all true.

But, you knew that didn't you?

You see, the more I think about it, the more I think, you had that chest in your house for all of those years and you probably even knew Uncle Abraham for a while when you were younger. He may have told you some things. Strange kind of things. Maybe you believed in this craziness all along. Maybe you gave that chest to Charlie because some weird stuff was starting to happen, like maybe some stuff in the chest was calling to you and trying to get you to do some pretty loopy stuff and so you thought the best thing you could do was send it to the other side of the ocean. But then, I've got to ask, why didn't you just burn the thing or ruin it somehow?

I'm guessing you couldn't.

It wouldn't let you, would it?

Just like Uncle Abraham couldn't scatter Dracula's ashes. Something stopped you from destroying it and so you did the next best thing. You dumped it on my brother.

Well, guess what. Charlie's resurrected Dracula.

I'm not joshing.

You may not know this, but he flew to Amsterdam and stole Dracula's urn from Uncle Abraham's coffin. Pretty gutsy move.

So, he brought the urn back and cast some spell he found in one of Abraham's books and whamo we have a vampire in our basement. Of course it wasn't as easy as that, and I myself don't know the ins and outs of it, but that's the gist.

Now, I'm sure you're wondering why he'd do something stupid like that. Well, he had this crazy idea to sic Dracula on Capone and his guys as payback for what they did to Pa.

Here's how it went down, but I'll tell you right now, it didn't go as planned.

I put some feelers out and learned that Capone was supposed to be at this warehouse just off the lake on the south side this past Friday. It's a pretty deserted neighborhood, especially at night. It seemed like a solid shot at getting to the big guy.

Now, you're probably wondering how Charlie dragged me into this scheme of his. Well, we're brothers. And there's no way he could handle Dracula by himself. And besides, it was me that got Pa killed. If something was to be done about it, I figure it's my responsibility.

Charlie made sure I saw it this way, but we don't need to go into that.

I can't even begin to tell you what Dracula's like. I guess a rabid dog says it best. All instinct. No speech. No memory as far as I can tell. We kept him chained all of the time and even that didn't seem like it was going to hold him much longer. It's as if he gets a little stronger every day. In case you missed it, that means he gets more difficult to control. In fact, we'd just had a pretty close call — both of us. So, the idea was to hurry up and use him on Capone and then kill him right after.

Pretty stupid, huh? We're thinking Capone's whole crew couldn't do the job, but that us two yahoos could just waltz in there and put him down after he'd done our dirty work. I guess we figured he'd be distracted or some other nonsense. Well, like I said, stupid.

Charlie came up with the idea to transport Dracula during the day. He's in a coma or something when the sun's up and it's the only time we can get close to him without being attacked. So, we put him in a crate, long and rectangular. We got to the warehouse a couple of hours before dusk. I'll tell you it wasn't easy because we took the box up a couple of flights of stairs that were on the outside of the building. The thing was heavy and we pretty much dragged it most of the way up to the roof. We even dropped it once. I kind of wish it'd broken open. Maybe Dracula would've just died in the sun and this whole thing would be a done deal.

But, once we got it to the top, it actually seemed like a pretty okay plan. There's this skylight window. We broke it with a pistol I'd brought to kill Dracula and reached in and unlocked it. This was all before Capone's people arrived.

So, here we were, waiting and waiting, and pretty soon the sun starts going down which is pretty much its habit. Well, now we start hearing sounds from inside the crate. Dracula's waking up. Swell. No sign of Capone or his guys yet.

Another half hour and the vampire's growling and kicking and whatnot. The crate's locked up pretty tight, but I'm afraid the commotion will scare the gangsters away when they finally show.

Finally, a car pulls up. And then a truck. It's Capone's guys. They drive right up to the building and get out of the vehicles. I recognize that gorilla-looking guy, Club, right off.

Club unlocks the door and they go in.

Charlie whispered, "I thought you said Capone was going to be here."

I shrugged. "Maybe he's still on his way."

Ten minutes later another truck pulled up. There're a bunch of crates in the bed. Liquor. The whole meeting was about a shipment. These were Capone's suppliers.

Charlie looked at me and said, "We Can't wait any longer. We don't want to kill those people."

He was right. We were there for Capone's crew. No one else. I nodded and then pulled out my pistol and shot a bullet into the sky.

The guys from the truck started hollering at each other and jumped back in the truck and took off. I could hear Capone's men inside shouting back and forth. The guns were already coming out. They thought they were under attack. Which they were, just not in any way they'd ever thought of.

We gave a good push on the crate and sent Dracula tumbling through the open window. The box hit the floor, shattering into a thousand pieces. All of the goons just stared at it, trying to figure out just what was going on.

Dracula practically jumped out of the shattered box, completely unharmed, angry as snot, and clamped his jaws on the closest man.

Everyone was screaming, but no one was shooting because the vampire was too close to their guy.

Blood spattered everywhere. I guess Dracula caught a major vein or something. He tossed the guy to the ground and jumped on another, biting him big on the neck. The guy tried to scream, but it was more of a gurgle. The other five guys started picking up planks of wood from the broken box and hitting him. I think they were still afraid to use their guns because they were all standing around in a circle.

With all of the commotion, police would be on their way soon and we didn't want to be stuck up top with no way to escape. So we ran down the outside stairs, the same way we'd gone up. Once on the ground, I peeked in a window. Uncle Hans, I ain't never seen so much blood. Dracula was covered in the stuff and by this point, there was only one other guy left alive. He pulled out his gun, but it was too late for that.

"Run!" I said to Charlie.

"No. We've got to kill the vampire."

"Get to the car. We can shoot him from the car." By this time I was pretty certain there was not going to be any easy way to kill that thing. I can't tell you how savage he was. Maybe like a wounded lion ripping apart lambs or something.

I never got to the car because I was only about half way across the gravel lot when I heard the shout. "Van Helsing!"

You hear the term, "my blood froze." Well, I think I know what they mean by that now. Hans, I've never been so scared.

I turned. I can't say why. Maybe I just felt I needed to see him if I was going to defend myself. Maybe his voice was so commanding that I had no choice. It was then that I realized Charlie hadn't followed me. He was just standing there gawking at Dracula. The two couldn't have been more than ten feet from each other.

The vampire was still naked and drenched in blood.

But he'd changed.

His hair wasn't white anymore and neither was his skin. The hair was now black as sin at midnight and his skin was as pink as a baby's butt after a spank or two. His face wasn't bony like it'd been, but was a little more rounded. And his eyes. They were intelligent and cold and mean.

It was the blood, I'm thinking. The human blood and so much of it. I think it made him young again and brought back his memories. Because he could talk now and he didn't act like any rabid dog. Even covered in blood and naked as an eel he stood there with some sort of wild dignity.

"Van Helsing," he said staring directly at Charlie while ignoring me as if I was a house pet. "You revived me and so I will not take you this night. Consider that small concession a debt paid. For when next we meet, I make no such promise."

And then he just turned and walked away. I never once thought to fire my gun. I don't even know if it would have worked on him, but I was just too dumbfounded to find out.

God, Uncle Hans, what have you brought to us?

Johnny

From the journal of Charles Van Helsing
March 27, 1930

It's been just under two weeks since we released Dracula on Capone's thugs. We missed our opportunity to get Capone and so he's still alive and well. We don't know why he wasn't there that night. Maybe Johnny was given bad information. Maybe Capone had a bad feeling about the place. Does it really matter? The good news is that, to our knowledge, he has no information connecting us to the attack on his men.

On another note, we've seen nothing of Dracula.

This troubles me to the core of my being.

Where is he? Who's he feeding on?

I can't tell you the guilt I feel, the terrible burden. Anyone killed by that beast may as well have been killed by my own hand. I brought this nightmare back into the world. I allowed him to escape. I've put lives at risk. I'm solely to blame for whatever may happen. I'm not even sure if I believe in heaven and hell, but if they exist, if all that we've been taught is real, well, if I wasn't damned before, I'm sure to be now.

From the journal of Charles Van Helsing
April 15, 1930

Over a month now and still no sign of Dracula. Johnny and I check the newspapers daily looking for evidence of him: bloodless corpses, actual sightings, anything unusual, but nothing obvious has appeared. I'm beginning to think that he's fled the country. This gives me some relief, though the guilt remains. Dracula is alive. Somewhere in this world he's feeding on people. It doesn't matter if it's here or abroad, I still bare the guilt of those lost lives and my despair increases daily for I unleashed a monster into the world for my own selfish reasons.

I think of things eternal now, things that barely tickled my mind until a month ago. Is there a God? Is there judgement to follow this life? If so, how can I be anything but damned? And is there still a path to redemption? Even if I was to kill Dracula today, wouldn't the weight of all of his victims still drag me into hell?

Oh, I could go on like this forever. Johnny, the wise and astute seventeen year-old, says I need to let these thoughts go, that they serve no purpose. But how can he truly know what I feel?

I suppose I should address another matter. Capone has shown no sign that he suspects us in the warehouse attack, and so I see no connection here, but he's continued expanding his operation, now into our territory, taking all of our clients. Every one of them. None are brave enough to refuse him. And honestly, I can't blame them. We've seen the consequences and I have no desire to lose another loved one.

So, at least for now, our bootlegging operations are finished. We're in the laundromat business again and nothing but. To be honest, it's a relief.

From the journal of Charles Van Helsing
May 2, 1930

It's happened. Dracula has attacked someone near to me.

It was late last evening and Mavis came to our door asking admittance. Mavis and I are still engaged, though we rarely see each other. We're betrothed in theory only. It's simply that neither of us has gotten around to making an official break. Maybe after Pop's been gone a while longer I'll pull the plug. The engagement was his idea, after all. I don't want to be disrespectful.

As to Mavis, though we've spent the last several weeks hunting the vampire, though I've read the journals and writings, though I know how Dracula used the woman, Mina Harker, when battling my great uncle, I was still surprised at how pale Mavis appeared. It just didn't register. Maybe I assumed it couldn't happen to us.

Like a fool, I asked about her health and she simply smiled and said, "Never better," before asking if we could speak in private.

In truth, I assumed she'd come by to break it off. But, Mavis hadn't come to end the relationship, at least not in any natural or human way. For as soon as we were alone in the living room, she scooted close to me on the couch and began touching me, running her fingers down my arms and then onto my chest, telling me how desirable I was. Her fingers found my hair. She stroked my head.

What was this, some sick joke? I knew how she felt about me. "What are you doing?" I asked as I attempted to scoot away.

She chuckled at my question and then put her lips to my neck, first kissing and then licking. Her tongue lingered and teased.

I don't care for Mavis and I know she feels the same toward me. But even so I felt glued to this place as if I was unable to refuse her advances.

My mind seemed to disengage.

Like it had under Dracula's influence.

I was barely aware as Mavis scratched me with her fingernail, drawing blood. It didn't seem the least bit unusual that she then licked my blood from her own fingertip and then from the skin of my neck. She cooed and licked, again scratching me. She put her lips to the scratches and began sucking. Her moans were of deep satisfaction and desire.

It was only Johnny's intervention that prevented something truly horrific from happening, for suddenly he was there holding, of all things, three garlic cloves he'd found in the kitchen.

Pulling away from me, Mavis gasped and then groaned a mournful growl.

Johnny advanced, the cloves outstretched.

Mavis's eyes went wide in horror and then, to my surprise, she fainted as if dead.

Johnny stared at the garlic and then at Mavis and then at the garlic again. "Well, damn," he said.

Realization struck me and I knelt beside Mavis, pulling back her collar to reveal two blood red puncture wounds on her neck.

From the journal of Vlad Dracula
May 2, 1930

It seems strange that I would so relish this journal, that I would take pains to return to the accursed basement to retrieve a mere book. But it has quite literally become a part of me. If not for the journal and the amazing properties I've imbued upon it I would still be mere dust. Even whatever minimal fragment of my being remained during those dark decades can be attributed to this tome. And so I will continue recording.

I suppose I should address those dark days of nonexistence, those many years that for all practicality I was dead to the living world. I have no memory of that time, I possessed no will, no intellect, no sense of self. All that was left of me was as a scrap separated from a greater self. The fact that in any tiny way I existed at all was the result of certain spells placed upon this journal more than a century before.

And so, when finally I came again into being in that dank and moldy basement, it was not with full cognizance or ability. No, I was just as I had been when first ushered into the eternal midnight. And so two Van Helsing brothers, relations to the Abraham Van Helsing so instrumental in my demise, were able to contain me with simple chains. But even during these unstable days, I had been able to impress upon the older brother, to nudge him into doing my will. For he has partaken of my blood and as such is forever mine.

Seeking revenge for their father's death, the brothers loosed me upon a group of ruffians and in doing so gave me the human blood needed for full recovery. This, of course, had been my intent, however unknown to my conscious mind, all along. Apparently my inner mind, my, what is the modern term? Subconscious. Apparently my subconscious is a devilish thing. In truth, after gorging myself on their enemies, I was ready to be done with the Van Helsings. I thought that I could be content to leave them to their own small and insignificant lives.

But, they are Van Helsings.

They carry the same blood as the despised Abraham.

And even Abraham showed me the respect of a worthy adversary. But these two! They chained me to a wall, fed me vermin, left me naked and exposed. How could I walk away from such as these and not seek recompense for such treatment? I would not be a man if I did such. There is yet a price to be paid in blood.

And so this leads me to Mavis Chandler, a striking young woman, the betrothed of Charles Van Helsing, the elder brother. Much as I had done with Mina Harker, the wife of Jonathan Harker, one of Abraham Van Helsing's allies, I have brought Mavis Chandler under my control.

The seduction was easy enough. The woman is of loose morals and frequents illegal establishments, usually unaccompanied by Van Helsing. This city is still largely unknown to me. It is heavily populated and located in America, an English speaking land across the Atlantic from Europe. The customs are peculiar, their use of language banal, but there is also a vibrancy which seems to endow the residents with vigor and expectation.

But I digress. Once learning of Mavis Chandler's connection to Van Helsing I determined her to be a perfect instrument and so followed her. Miss Chandler entered a so-called speakeasy with two giggling and vacuous female companions. I waited several minutes and then, through simple persuasion, coaxed the doorkeeper to bid me entrance.

The room was small, dark, and smoke filled. Most persons were at some level of inebriation and it seemed the type of establishment where men and women gathered to flirt and cavort. I found Miss Chandler talking with a tall young man of about twenty-five.

The male was easily dismissed as I caught Miss Chandler's eye and beckoned her with subtle words. To her, I appeared foreign and exotic. Certainly she assumed I was a man of means for since departing the Van Helsings I have acquired fine garments and appropriate grooming to reflect my true stature as a nobleman. The woman giggled and pawed at me, frequently brushing against me in a disgusting display of wanton lust.

The establishment was dark and smoke filled. I had no need to depart with the woman. We stood only perhaps five feet distant from another couple, arms wrapped about one another, as I bent, first whispering into her ear, and then biting ever so delicately into the tender flesh of her neck. She offered a soft sigh, nearly a coo, pulling closer to me as I drew her life fluid.

Oh, I cannot tell you of the ecstasy of this contact. I had fed on rats. And before that I had been as nothing, only a phantom thought, barely that. But these past days, drinking the essence of human life, refreshing my limbs with that vital fluid. Oh, it took all of the control I could muster to restrain from draining her to death. Such exquisite moments.

After several seconds, I drew away, scratched my own neck with a nail, and then forced her lips to the open wound. She offered only minimal resistance before drawing deeply of my blood. Miss Chandler now belongs to me. The game, I believe, should be quite interesting.

From the journal of Charles Van Helsing
May 3, 1930

Let me tell you about Earl Chandler. Mavis's father is a small man with large eyeglasses and the perpetual look of bewilderment on his slightly puffy face. To say that he is gnome-like would be over complimentary. His shoulders are rolled, his hair thin, and his head speckled with warts and moles. The fact that he was able to produce such a stunning daughter has always confounded me. But I'm pretty sure she's really his daughter. The resemblance is in the lips and eyes.

Earl came pounding on our door early this morning, all full of bluster and indignation, demanding to see Mavis and accusing me of defiling her virtue. He actually used that term, defiling her virtue. It took Johnny and me several minutes to calm him and it was only when we led him to her, asleep and alone in our spare bedroom, that he settled some.

It was obvious that she was very sick and Earl couldn't help but see this. "We couldn't send her home last night," I explained. "She's too weak. And to be honest, we couldn't explain what was wrong with her on the telephone. You wouldn't have believed it without seeing her in person."

He was full of questions, none of which had easy answers. Explaining to a worried father that his daughter's been bitten by a vampire takes some finesse.

Of course he was skeptical. But we couldn't allow him to take Mavis home. There was just too much risk. At least Johnny and I understood what we were facing. We've seen Dracula. We know his savagery. And, through reading my ancestor's collection of writings, we at least have some idea of how to combat the thing.

It took some convincing but eventually Earl agreed to let her stay. And so would he. "If by the end of the night I don't see anything to prove you two aren't soft in the head, I'm taking her away and you'll never see Mavis or our money again," he said.

I was fine with this proposition.

My mother was another issue. How were we supposed to explain to her why we wouldn't let Earl take Mavis home, not to mention why we were placing garlic cloves throughout the guest bedroom? I feared telling her the truth knowing that the shock might finally kill her. And so I was completely flabbergasted when she looked up from her seat by the window and said, "Charlie, when are you going to tell me about your vampire?"

Johnny and I looked at each other in astonishment and then back at her.

"You boys can close your mouths before you start catching flies." She smiled.

"Ma," said Johnny. "There ain't no vampire. What are you talking about?"

"Ain't isn't a real word, son, and do you honestly believe I don't know that Abraham's story is real? Do you really think I don't know why there's garlic strung all over that bedroom or what you were hiding in the basement?"

At this point, I stepped forward. "Why didn't you say anything?"

"Because I just don't have the energy to fight with you boys. I'll tell you, I was terrified while that beast was here. I don't know how you came to have that thing, but I was hoping you'd killed it. I suppose that was too much to ask for."

"It's not just any vampire," I said. "It's Dracula, the one Abraham fought."

She seemed to contemplate this. "And Mavis?" asked Mom. "Is he trying to get to you through her, Charlie? Of course he is. He's a crafty devil, that one." She paused another moment and then turned, reaching for her jewelry box atop her end table. "I suppose you're going to need some crosses. I don't have any crucifixes, we're not Catholic, but I have two or three crosses on necklaces. I'd think they'll work just as well. Put these in the room with Mavis. According to the Stoker book, they should do something."

I felt an amazing swell of love for my mother in that moment. I'd thought her weak and I'd been wrong. She was ill and she was grieving, but it would be a mistake to ever think of her as weak. I'll remember that from now on.

From the journal of Charles Van Helsing
May 4, 1930

Things couldn't have gone worse.

Mavis grew increasingly agitated as evening drew near. She didn't speak at all and rarely even opened her eyes. The room was heavy with the smell of garlic. We'd placed one of Mom's cross necklaces around Mavis's neck, another hanging before the window, and another looped over the corner of the mirror. I had no true hope in these, no faith that the supremacy of God would manifest in these metal charms, but still, at some level, wished for some hint that there was some power greater than the evil we faced.

Earl paced back and forth throughout the day continually announcing that it was only out of respect for our father that he put up with this foolishness. He didn't shut up until Mom hobbled into the room, met his gaze and said, "You're acting like an idiot, Earl. The boys know what they're doing. Either be a help or shut up and get out."

Earl flushed, pushed his glasses up with an index finger, and said, "Anne, I don't mean to upset you…"

"Then don't. Make yourself useful and go fix me some tea. It's going to be a long night."

Ignoring him, she then made her way to Mavis, sat on the corner of the bed, and examined the pale young woman. Earl stood dumbly for a moment, adjusted his glasses again, and then exited the room. A few minutes later he returned carrying a cup of tea.

We spent the next hour bringing Mom and Earl up to speed on the resurrection of Dracula, the revenge on Capone's cronies, and of Dracula's escape. We left out any reference to the raid on Capone's shipment that had led to Pop's murder.

We'd all been up throughout the day, and it was unlikely we could stay awake all night to guard Mavis. And so we decided to take shifts. Johnny would sit with her first, Earl second, and then me. Mom was too weak to contribute in this way and so retired to her room.

It was clear that Earl still had his doubts. In retrospect, we should have realized this and not trusted him to guard Mavis alone. But she was his daughter. I guess neither of us felt we had the right to refuse him.

Somewhere during Earl's shift, maybe one A.M., he succumbed to sleep. I can only guess that Dracula had been waiting for this opportunity. It seems he came to the window and instructed Mavis to remove the garlic and crosses because we found these in a heap just outside of the bedroom door.

Earl awoke just as the vampire entered through the now open window.

I heard his shout from my room. Johnny and I entered the hallway simultaneously, charging into the small guest bedroom just in time to see Dracula hurl Earl against the wall mirror causing it to shatter.

Dracula was much changed. He was fashionably dressed in the style of the day, with a fine pinstriped suit, patent leather shoes, and expensive wristwatch. His coal black hair was now trimmed short and slicked back from his high forehead. He wore a narrow mustache and his cheeks were flushed pink, most likely due to the blood of a recent victim coursing through his veins. His face was vital, his features nearly youthful. He seemed three decades younger than he had when chained in our basement. I guess that's what a diet of human blood will do.

Our eyes met and I felt a strange vibration race down my spine. That gaze. That incredible will.

Dracula drew the semi catatonic Mavis into a firm hug.

Johnny rushed forward, a long kitchen knife raised as if to strike. Dracula slapped him aside with barely a thought.

I couldn't move. Dear God, I couldn't move. Not even a twitch. I wanted to, wanted nothing more than to send this filthy beast back to hell, to destroy him again, to return him to ashes, but for some terrifying reason my feet just wouldn't obey my commands. Maybe I was just too frightened to move. Maybe it was simple fear. I truly hope so because I'd rather think of myself as the worst conceivable coward than to consider the other implications.

Dracula smiled.

I stared, mute and useless.

Johnny scrambled to his feet as Earl staggered forward, still shaky from Dracula's attack. But Dracula was already moving through the window, pulling Mavis along with him. They disappeared like vapor into the night.

Mavis is gone. We'll probably never see her alive again.

From The Chicago Tribune
May 12, 1930

Chicago – Four bloodless bodies were discovered early this morning along the lakefront just south of Lincoln Park. This brings the total of such bodies to over twenty. Detective Walter O'Malley of the Chicago Police Department says they still have no clues as to the cause of this strange phenomenon. City officials refuse to speculate on the cause of the deaths but call the rumors of vampires nonsense and fiction.

Document found in the home of Clyde Moore
dated May 13, 1930

To whom it may concern,

I am writing this as I am preparing to embark on a peculiar endeavor. Ah, you say I am always involved in the peculiar. And, so I agree, this is so. But, in this, I have a sense of terrible things. To be specific, I have been asked to aid in a hunt of sorts. Yes, yes, this may sound strange to the ears, for none who know me would think me the hunter. Ah, but this hunt is of an uncanny nature, dreadful and mystical. I and my companions seek to capture and then slay a beast of significant power and intellect. A creature from beyond the veil who has manifested himself on this earth.

And now this to the point. Should I not return, no blame should be placed on the young gentlemen Charles and Jonathan Van Helsing, or one Earl Chandler. I participate of my own will. My dear, dear niece, Pearl, who loves me much more than I deserve, of course is guiltless as well. Oh, I seek to convince her to step aside, to stay far away from this task, but her tenacity, the adventurous spirit of the youth, this causes her to insist on the danger. My hope is that I will soon share with you the tale of this great hunt, but this is a perilous task and so the outcome is uncertain.

Another matter, and this of importance. I know that many believe I consulted with devils and that these terrors granted me my wealth before forcing me to flee my beloved Haiti. While it is true that I have had contact with spirits both benevolent and foul, and that it was indeed some of these forces that led to my flight, I must reassure all that I never intended to betray a trust. My goal, despite my methods, was always the betterment of my people. Yes, yes, you may find this difficult to accept, but my words are true. I have lived with a heavy soul for these many years since departing my dear country. And I hope by putting an end to this present demon, that I might in some small way redeem myself in your eyes.

Clyde Moore known to my countrymen as Clajames Selvandieu

Letter from Johnny Van Helsing to Hans Van Helsing
May 16, 1930

Hans,

This is getting real serious. Bloodless corpses are being found all over Chicago and Charlie's fiancée, Mavis, has been missing for two weeks now. No sign of her or Dracula. I thought her dad, Earl, was going to shoot Charlie when he learned the whole story of Dracula's rebirth. But I stepped in, used some finesse. You know Charlie, brains and brawn, but no finesse. Earl's with us now, but he blames Charlie. And Charlie blames me for Pa. We're all just happy partners.

Yeah. Of course we are.

But let me get on with it. I'm spooked. And not just about the vampire anymore. Charlie went to this uncle and niece named Clyde and Pearl for help on account of Clyde being in the know on supernatural stuff. Clyde's a freakish little fella. He's what Pearl calls a bokor. I guess that basically means witch doctor. He's from Haiti and talks with a pretty strong accent. I don't know about any bokors, but he's just plain irregular.

The house has strange smells. Pearl called them incense and I have no cause to doubt her. There are thick black curtains over all of the windows so even in the daylight the place is dark like a crypt. And no furniture. Nothing to sit on but woven mats on the floor.

So, we show up at his place. Pearl's uncle wore no shirt, black trousers, and no shoes. His skin is black as midnight but gleams in the light like maybe he's covered in sweat or oil or something. His head was shaved bald and he had some weird symbol painted on the top of his skull. Clyde – what a normal name for such an oddball guy, huh?

But Pearl adores him. Her face just had this big glow about it when she looked at him, so I figured no matter how weird, he couldn't be all bad. Pearl, she's okay. More than okay really. Charlie likes her. And I think I'm liking her too.

Clyde greeted us each by name, his smile big and toothy. "Charlie, so good to see you. And the young one, Johnny, of course you are. And Earl, the missing lady's father. We will do all that we can. Come in, come in."

He quizzed Charlie on the resurrection of Dracula for more than an hour. Finally, after Charlie had told him everything for what seemed a dozen times, Clyde nodded and said, "This is a powerful creature you have unleashed, with powerful magics. Slaying him will be no simple task."

"We already know he's powerful," said Earl, who looked even more uncomfortable then me. "But let's get to the nitty gritty. How do we kill it and get my daughter back?"

Clyde, he just looked at Earl for a little while and then let out a kind of a sigh. "My dear friend, you must understand this is not an easy thing you ask. How do we kill a vampire? There are many answers, but the true question is how do we kill this vampire? For there are many vampiric forms and not all of the same origin. And this one has used incantations and spells beyond his original transformation in order to live yet again."

I could tell Earl was about to shoot off his mouth and say something entirely unhelpful. He's not a real religious man, but he has some of it in him, and I think Mavis's abduction has caused more of that to come up on top. He didn't like the idea of going to see Clyde with all of his voodoo stuff. He thought maybe a priest would be better. But to be honest about the thing, I think Earl was hiding behind his religion and that his real problem had more to do with Clyde being colored. He'd said things along the way like, "I've never been to a Negro house before," and "How is this Negro supposed to help me get my daughter back." Pearl was in the back seat and somehow managed to keep from smacking Earl on account of his dumb-headed comments. I kind of like her for it. For, you know, rising above this ignoramus and not letting him bate her. The lady has some class.

Anyway, before Earl could shoot his mouth at Clyde, Pearl jumped in and kind of coaxed Clyde along. "Clyde, why don't you tell him some basic ways to kill a vampire? Then we can get more specific, huh?"

"Ah," said Clyde. "I understand your worries. Trust me, my friend, my wish is to help you bring this beast back to his grave. But to kill the vampire is not an easy thing. Cut off its head, this will do it, but how do you get close enough? And if you do cut off the head, the garlic has power. It may seem a strange thing but garlic has strong magic against the vampire. Place the clove in the mouth of the severed head and you may prevent the reattachment. A knife or a stake through the heart will kill the thing, but maybe not permanently. And if the blade has been given magic, then your chances are so much the better. Sunlight is your finest weapon, but how do you get the vampire into the sun? Fire will kill the beast, but it takes long and if the creature is not brought to ash he may heal. And this vampire, ah! He has already been ash and yet he walks the night. What are we to assume of such a creature?"

"What about the cross?" asked Earl.

Clyde grinned. "The cross, the crucifix, yes, these may be of help. Not to kill, but to contain. Some vampires are susceptible to this, but not all. Understand this. Dracula, as a man, subscribed to the Christian faith. And so this symbol, maybe still it holds some influence."

"Then what do we do?" This time it was Charlie. "My Uncle Abraham and his friends killed him once, there must be a way to do it again."

"Yes. And some of their methods, these are the same as I have mentioned. But, think with me. Is this the same Dracula that they defeated or has he been transformed? No, no. think, please. Has he not died and then invoked some powerful magics to resurrect? Will he still fall before the same things that killed him before?"

Earl pushed at his glasses with a finger and said, "So you're no use to us at all."

Clyde lowered his tone. "Please, friend. Do not presume so much. We all here have the same goal. I only mean to tell you the plain truth of this thing. Now, let us begin. You have brought the cross, I see. And I assume the knife and the bullets."

Charlie nodded. Clyde had instructed him to bring these things.

What happened after that was very irregular. When Clyde took the bag holding the weapons from Charlie, he stopped and put his palm on Charlie's cheek. Looking at him in some real intense way, he said. "May all of the good spirits guard your soul, my friend." And then he turned to me and leaned in real close and said in a whisper so only I could hear, "Your responsibility is to your wife to be. Always protect her. Do not forget."

And then he turned away and took us to the kitchen where he was boiling different roots in big black pots. Without saying another word, he put the cross, the knives, the bullets, all into these pots. Charlie asked him why he did this and he said, "The roots, they have great *ashe*, or power. I use their properties and some incantations to make your weapons strong."

"Wait," said Earl. "You're putting a spell on the cross? That can't be proper."

Clyde just gave a peculiar wide-eyed look and said, "The bokor serves the *loa* with both hands."

"What's that supposed to mean?" asked Earl.

Pearl looked at him and said, "It means they use both light magic and black magic."

Earl looked like he'd just swallowed a squirrel and I knew from that point on, no matter what happened, this was not going to end in any way good.

Wish you were here, Hans. It was you that started it and now I think you're afraid to tackle it.

Write back, will you?

Johnny

From The Amsterdam Recorder
May 29, 1930

Amsterdam – Fifty-three year-old Hans Van Helsing was found late yesterday by his wife, Aleen Van Helsing, dead by apparent suicide. Mrs. Van Helsing told officials that she had returned home from their daughter's home to find her husband missing. After searching the residence, she then discovered him in the shed where he hung by noose from a rafter. A note was found in Mr. Van Helsing's chest pocket. It said only, "God spare my soul." Mrs. Van Helsing was not available for comment, but did tell police that her husband had been troubled lately by disturbing correspondences from a relative overseas.

From the journal of Charles Van Helsing
June 10, 1930

We killed our first vampire tonight. It wasn't Dracula and we didn't escape without incident or injury. We've been quite busy over the past weeks tracking strange deaths and unusual sightings, questioning witnesses, scanning newspapers, patrolling areas near recent incidents. We've even used Clyde's magic to discover disturbances in the supernatural domain, or whatever he calls it. And this helped us to locate this particular vampire. But we've yet to find Dracula's hideout or any evidence as to Mavis's whereabouts.

And let's not forget who unleashed Dracula. All of this: Mavis, the multiple deaths around the city, all my fault.

In case you were wondering, I don't sleep very well these days.

The vampire was animalistic, near mindless, nothing but instinct. Obviously, she was in the early days of her new existence and hadn't yet come back into her mind or memories. As we'd wrongly assumed that Dracula was the only vampire terrorizing the city, we were shocked to find her. Obviously, he's made another. We can only hope that this was the only one.

We used our tools against her: garlic, stakes, knives, crosses, but avoided using guns because the sound would draw attention.

Following Clyde's lead, we'd found her in an alleyway feasting on a young man of about her own age, which we put at about twenty. I can tell you in all truthfulness that to a person we were terrified as we stepped away from the safety of the lighted thoroughfare and into the shadows to face this creature.

The vampire snarled as we approached, dropping her now dead victim to the ground. She crouched, her head angling as she sniffed the air. Clyde shouted some strange incantation and Earl threw holy water he'd gotten from a priest. Earl doesn't trust Clyde or his bizarre mystical methods and chooses to rely on his own, more familiar spirituality.

Clyde's incantation seemed of little use and Earl's holy water did nothing but annoy the beast. We tried our best to encircle her, but the vampire kept her back to the wall, using it as a defense, and charging out at us with bared fangs whenever we approached.

Gradually, we closed the circle, each of us holding a stake or a knife that had been chanted over by Clyde. These weapons seemed entirely inadequate for the task and I can tell you right now that though the weapons prayed over by Clyde had a peculiar tingling warmth to the touch, I still held no true hope that any of his incantations would help.

I really hoped to be proven wrong.

Even more, I wished we'd had a gun.

Or maybe a canon.

But a gunshot would draw attention. We could very easily be charged with murder if we were seen gunning down what to others would seem a poor unfortunate girl.

But this was no girl. Her eyes were red with the fires of hell, her elongated teeth were red with the blood of her victim. She hissed and growled and drooled like a rabid beast.

We tightened the circle, closer. The vampire lunged toward Earl. He skipped back, just avoiding her. Pearl stabbed with her knife, catching the vampire on the arm. The monster hissed and was about to leap at Pearl when I cut it on the left shoulder blade. It whirled, its attention now on me. My knife had cut through her skin like butter. Was this the effect of Clyde's magic, or simply the mark of a sharp knife? I still don't know.

Let me pause for an explanation. Something happened with Clyde in Haiti. According to Pearl, he used some particularly strong magic, maybe summoning spirits of some kind to cure a sickness in his village. But he couldn't control the phantoms he'd released. A lot of people died. Apparently, he was banished after that and came to the States. Pearl says he's now very careful about his magic, that maybe there are stronger spells, but he refuses to risk something like that again. I can't blame him, but I'm afraid we needed the heavy artillery for this.

Clyde shouted another incantation. I attempted a low stab, but missed. Earl jabbed, catching the vampire in the left side this time. Pearl's not shy and she's not timid, not the type to stand in the background and let the men do all of the work. So she was right in there with us, taking a wild swing, clipping the vampire's ear. Johnny then moved in for the kill.

The vampire was too quick for him.

I can't describe how fast it happened, but in an instant she'd pulled Johnny forward, thrust his blade to the side, and pressed her fangs into the flesh of his neck.

Horrified, I jumped on her, catching her off balance, and pulling her to the gravel surface. I guess personal safety is forgotten at such times. I could think of nothing but getting that thing off of Johnny as I stabbed and stabbed and stabbed. That beast would not have my brother.

Pearl wrenched Johnny free, Clyde mumbled spells, Earl, like me, stabbed. But he was less frenzied, more precise. I've said before that Earl is a small man, that he reminds me of a gnome, but here I saw an inner strength that I hadn't suspected. Pushing the vampire's flailing arms aside, he thrust his blade directly into her chest, penetrating the heart.

A surprising quantity of blood shot upward from the damaged organ, speckling Earl's face and glasses.

The vampire stopped. Instantly. Her eyes went wide and then went from the dark crimson near black of the vampire to the cornflower blue they'd obviously been in life. She sighed once, a tiny curl of a grin whisking over her bloodied lips, and then she was dead.

Clyde immediately shoved a garlic clove into her mouth and began the process of ritual decapitation while I scrambled away to where Pearl cradled Johnny in her lap.

"Johnny! Johnny!" I screamed as I dropped to my knees beside them.

"He's alright, I think," said Pearl as she gently stroked his hair. "He was bitten, but only just. And she didn't have a chance to make him drink any of her blood."

I nodded, moving my head to within inches of his. "Johnny?"

He offered a weak grin. "Hurts like hell. But, hey how many fellas can say they've been bitten by a vampire?" He tried to chuckle, but I could see that it pained him.

"You're a brat," I said through a relieved smile.

"And you're a klutz. All of that stabbing and not one to the heart. Glad I don't have to rely on you."

I gave him a gentle punch to the bicep.

We both grinned.

Pearl stroked his hair.

Johnny reached up, squeezed her hand.

I felt a twinge of irrational jealousy, but dismissed it. She was simply comforting him. And after what he'd just experienced, I had no right to any feeling but thankfulness that he was alive.

From the journal of Charles Van Helsing
June 29, 1930

We're at Earl's house, which I guess has become our unofficial meeting place. Earl's sent his wife to a sister's house for safety and he's got more space than we have at our little place. Duke Ellington is playing on the phonograph. Pearl's in the next room reading her latest must-read novel, something called *A Farewell to Arms*. Earl, Clyde, and Johnny are outside tinkering with Earl's automobile. I'm at the dining room table.

Our group is quite peculiar. Earl still distrusts Clyde's mysticism but the two have found an awkward sort of comradery and often I find them in each other's company. I think Earl's unease at Clyde's color has diminished as they've spent time together. As well, Johnny and Pearl have become nearly inseparable. I have no claim on Pearl's affections. We are after all on a mission to save my fiancée. She's only two years older than my brother and they have a surprising amount of things in common. But I can't help but feel a twinge each time I see them laughing or in deep conversation.

We've successfully killed three vampires now. These were all young in what Dracula calls the eternal midnight. Clyde tells us that Dracula will be a much more difficult kill, that he has full intellect and powerful spells protecting him. I know some of this is assumption. Dracula alluded to certain enchantments and precautions in his journal, but never detailed these. We really don't know what, if any, additional powers he might have gained, but I guess it's smart to assume that he'll be the most difficult kill.

There was some discussion as to why Dracula had made these vampires. To our knowledge he'd never before created other beasts indiscriminately, but only when he sought a companion. Johnny offered the most likely motive saying, "Distractions. If there are vampire attacks all over the city, we never know when it's him or one of the others."

It made sense. Our strategy had been to track the location of each attack and by doing this narrow our search for his hideaway to the area of the attacks. At which point Clyde can use his voodoo to pinpoint the vampire. The growing vampire population has made our task much more difficult. I really wish Dracula had done us a favor and just stayed a mindless beast. Call me lazy, but I'm really not swell on the idea of tracking a crafty monster.

I guess I should stop now. Dusk is only four hours away and I need some sleep before the night's hunt.

Had I mentioned that my life's become just plain peculiar?

From the journal of Vlad Dracula
July 13, 1930

I have now read the book compiled from Abraham Van Helsing's collection of documents and have seen what he truly thought of me. A child mind, he said. I had lived for centuries before his birth and he had the audacity to compare me to a child. The man was a self-important fool with his wrong-headed assumptions about me and my kind. So much of what he treated as fact about the nosferatu had little or no basis in truth.

And this leads me to another issue. The descendants, the brothers. I fight with myself concerning their fates. As a person of honor, I feel compelled to offer some small leniency to the one who brought me back into existence. But my instinct is to slay them. Ah, the heart is a trickster, ever teasing me with contradictions. How I sometimes wish that I was the mindless monster some suppose me to be, that I had that child mind of Van Helsing's delusions, that I could act on instinct alone and not suffer the indignities of honor and conscience.

But, I prattle.

The truth of it is this: the Van Helsing brothers and their companions will not rest until they find and destroy me. Therefore I am left with no choice but to go on the offensive.

And so again I utilize the wanton fiancée. Certainly it is she they seek, likely more than they do me. Clearly it was a mistake to take her. Admittedly, I can be impulsive and the abduction of this girl has done nothing but to give these people a motivation. And so I will give them that which they desire. They will receive Mavis Chandler. And when they do this thing will be very near to an end.

From the journal of Charles Van Helsing
July 14, 1930

Dracula's playing with us.

Of course he's playing with us. He's intelligent. He's lived for centuries. He knows we're after him and he's tossing vampires at us like confetti in a tickertape parade. He's most likely watching us from the shadows as we blindly follow clue after clue only to again discover that we've tracked another of his baby vamps.

It was late, or early, I guess. Three A.M. Clyde and Pearl had gone to Clyde's place to resupply; the rest of us remained in Earl's kitchen. Earl produced three bottles of German beer from a box beside the refrigerator and gave Johnny and me one each. Johnny sat on the counter, I was leaning against the wall, and Earl took a seat at the oak table which was the centerpiece of the room. He adjusted his glasses with a nudge from his index finger, took a deep sip of beer, and gazed off into what seemed to be nothingness.

"We'll find her," said Johnny.

Earl continued to study the unknown depths of the wall.

"Honest," said Johnny. "She's out there."

"Is she?" asked Earl. "How can you know that?"

Johnny stammered, but had no reply.

"I know you're trying to say the things you think I need to hear. But, do you really think we'll find her? And if we do, what are the chances that she'll still be my little girl?"

Johnny stared at Earl for a moment and then said, "I don't know. I mean, I want her to be."

"What about you?" Earl was now looking at me. "Do you really think she's still alive and well?"

I met his gaze. "Honestly, I hope he's keeping her alive as a hostage, as something to trade for his freedom if we ever catch him. That's the only reason I can see him keeping her human." I took a swig of beer. Bitter, nearly as bitter as my soul. "I'm sorry," I said. "I never wanted anything to happen to her."

Earl released a half laugh half scoff as he shook his head. "You never loved her. The engagement was all about money."

I moved from the wall and seated myself in the chair across from Earl. "No. I didn't love her. We had nothing in common. That doesn't mean I'd want something to happen to her."

Earl sipped long on his beer, nudged his glasses. "Did you hear it? Did you hear what you just did?"

He paused, waiting for a response. I had no idea what he was talking about.

"Past tense," said Earl at last. "You talked about my baby in the past tense." His voice broke on the final word. He turned away, obviously trying to hide the emerging tears. I sat there dumbly, with no idea of how to respond, the fiancé that didn't love the girl, the revenge crazed man who'd put her at risk to begin with.

Johnny slid off of the counter, setting his beer down, and moving to Earl. He put a hand on the man's back, patted. A comforting gesture, something I never would have thought to do.

Earl shrugged him off. "No. Just go. Okay? Just go home."

Johnny stepped back, stared at Earl, and then nodded. Rising silently, I followed my seventeen year-old brother into the living room and then through the front doorway, never saying another word to the agonized man. This is my fault. All of it. And I seriously doubt I'll ever be able to live with myself again.

From The Chicago Tribune
July 15, 1930

Chicago – City officials are set to meet today to address the so-called vampire murders. Though the name of this spree is inspired by the mythical creature, police are adamant that these brutal attacks have nothing to do with monsters of the night, but are more likely connected to organized crime. It has now been revealed that the first such attack was perpetrated in an abandoned warehouse against men believed to be connected to Al Capone. Though none of the other thirty-nine victims have a known connection to the mob, it is still thought that these murders are meant to send some sort of message to rival factions. One source indicates that Capone believes the attack to have been perpetrated by Bugs Moran as retaliation to last year's St. Valentine's Day Massacre...

From the journal of Charles Van Helsing
July 16, 1930

Dear God, the worst has happened. It's only because I believe it's important to leave a record of these events that I even attempt to write these words. Forgive my shaky hand, but I can barely control my own muscles.

We were all at Earl's house, Johnny and I were in the kitchen, Clyde and Pearl on the couch sipping tea, Earl in the corner talking with his wife on the telephone. There was a knock at the door. Earl hung up the telephone, marched across the room, and answered the door. It was Mavis.

Her skin was like porcelain, her teeth white as a fresh snow, elongated and fierce, her eyes, midnight crimson.

I think we all acted at once, shouting at Earl to close the door. But this was his missing daughter and he did what any father would do, falling into her arms, tears of joy racing down his cheeks, a moan that could have been deep joy or abject loss rising from his breast. "Mavis, oh my baby. We can be together again."

For an instant I thought she might have mercy on him, that some still human spark might cause her to spare her own father. She wrapped her arms about him, stroked his head, gazed into his eyes. And then she grabbed his shirt collar and, with inhuman strength, dragged him onto the front lawn and sank her teeth into his flesh. The deed was done before the rest of us had clamored to snatch our weapons.

By the time we reached the lawn they'd disappeared into the night, enveloped by an unnatural mist. The entire encounter had taken less than a minute. We spread out, racing up the street, through adjacent lawns, between buildings, onto the next block, but there was no evidence of them whatsoever.

Thinking about it now, I'm certain the mist must have originated with Dracula. Mavis is a new vampire, several weeks at the most. It's unlikely she'd be capable of conjuring the mist. And the night was clear, both before and after the encounter. This was not a natural phenomenon. The fiend had been close. Nearly within our grasp. But hidden. Always hidden. How many times has he stood in the wings, watching from the shadows as we battle his fledgling vampires? Laughing, leading us this way and that, toying with us.

But what of Earl? Another lost soul for my conscience to bear. Another damnation card for Charlie. We lost one of our own tonight without even the chance to fight for him. And now it comes to me. Now I get it. The one thing we'd never allowed ourselves to consider. We may not win this war with Dracula. There is no preordained outcome with us the victors. There's no guarantee that we'll survive. The game has shifted. We'd foolishly assumed ourselves to be the hunters.

But we are the prey.

I can only wonder which one of us will be next.

From the journal of Johnny Van Helsing
July 27, 1930

I'm starting this diary because someone's got to keep a record of this stuff. You can read Charlie's journal for all the background up to this point. He kept a pretty exact record.

This is hard for me. This is really hard for me. So I think I'm just going to try to plow through it. You know, just tell what happened and keep the emotions out of the works.

I guess there's no way to start but with this: Dracula came to our house.

It was four nights ago. After Earl was attacked at his place, none of us really felt comfortable there anymore so we started meeting at our house. Honestly, after that, we didn't know what to do. We kept hunting for Dracula, but had no clues. I think we all felt he could just come after us anytime he wanted. Which is what he did.

It was early evening. We were still making our plans for the night. Pearl had been at our house for a while already and Clyde had just got there. Ma was there too. Still frail as a baby with a bottle, but spunky. Ma was always spunky in spirit even if her body was all shivers and groans.

We had a map of the city laid out on the coffee table in the living room. Ma was in her rocking chair, not participating, just listening. Pearl was sitting next to me on the couch and Clyde was in a chair across from us. Charlie was leaning against the wall, all silent and brooding. It was like something was bothering him.

Something from the inside. It almost seemed like he was fighting with himself, shaking his head sometimes or grunting. He was just plain distracted.

They came in through the windows, the vampires, just breaking right through them.

It was Dracula, Mavis, and Earl. All three of them were full vampires, but Earl, he was the newest one and so he was still animal-like. All beast, no brain.

They say vampires can't come into a place unless they've been invited. I don't know if that's true or not. If it is, I figure all three of these vamps had been here before. Mavis and Earl when they were human, and Dracula both when he was resurrected and when Mavis invited him in after that. So, maybe that counted. I guess that doesn't really matter. They were there and just like at Earl's place, we were caught unprepared.

There was a moment of shock where we all just stood there, nobody knowing what to do. Dracula looked at each of us. His eyes were real intense and it seemed like he stared at Charlie longer than the rest of us. And then he said in this perfect British accent, "It is important for you to know that I do only what you have forced me to do. Though you are Van Helsings, I had inclinations to let you live and have debated on how best to proceed. My only goal, you see, was to exist undisturbed and in anonymity. But you've taken that option from me."

It almost sounded like he might have had regret in his tone, like maybe he wanted some other way, but then he nodded once and the attack was on. If we'd acted quicker, maybe we could have stopped some of what happened next. But I don't think so. Things were just too out of control.

Earl went after Ma. She was the closest to the window and she was slow. It wasn't that she didn't put up a fight. She batted him with her cane and slapped and punched. Pearl and me raced to them, both of us trying to pull Earl off her, but I could already see the blood. God, there was a lot of blood.

"Ma!" I cried. "Ma!" I just kept screaming it over and over.

We had our knives and stakes in the room. Pearl grabbed Earl by the hair and I stabbed him about five or six times in the back. He whirled around, dropping Ma, and clawed at me with his fingernails, which, by the way, were now long and sharp. Pearl tried to stab him too, but Mavis grabbed her and threw her against the side of the couch. She wasn't hurt, just winded.

Earl was hurt, though, but not dead.

I stabbed Earl one last time, right in the chest. That did it. He was down. Dead but not dead. If the knife was pulled out, he'd get back up, but as long as we left the knife in till we could decapitate him or burn him, he'd stay dead.

Mavis grabbed me by the neck.

I didn't have a knife because mine was sticking out of Earl's chest.

Mavis bit me, right there in the neck the way they do, but suddenly she screeched as Charlie half stumbled to her, stabbing her in the back of the neck.

Everything was berserk. Mavis let go of me screaming and then started trying to pull the knife from her neck.

Charlie stood there all confused on his face.

I saw Pearl run past me to the kitchen. "I have an idea," she said, but this really didn't sink in till later.

Clyde was facing down Dracula, but I didn't have a good look at what was happening just then.

"Are you okay?" asked Charlie. He had a strange upset look like maybe he was ready to vomit.

"Yeah, yeah. Just another vampire bite. No biggie." It was a biggie, but I wasn't about to say anything.

Charlie squinted, like he was in pain or something, and shook his head. When he spoke his voice was small like maybe he was struggling to talk. "Johnny, be serious. I don't know how much longer I'll be me." He put his hand on my shoulder, all concerned. He was shaking and sweating. Something was very wrong with him.

And then he pulled me forward, almost to where he could kiss me. "I'm proud of you," he said in this strained kind of voice. And then his eyes just went blank, like maybe his brain went on vacation. And he moved away from me, shaking his head and mumbling. I wanted to go to him, to slap him or something, try to pull him out of it. But whatever was going on with Charlie would have to wait because things were berserk all around us. Now I wish I'd taken his behavior more seriously. I wish I'd done something. Anything!

Mavis was twirling in circles, making weird gawking sounds and still trying to get the knife out of her neck. Clyde was backing Dracula down with a cross and a knife. He was chanting his voodoo stuff and I think it was working some because Dracula seemed slow and maybe a little dazed or even in pain, like maybe something was twisting around inside him. He was backed against the wall and Clyde had his blade raised to strike.

I was just bending to grab a knife when I heard a gunshot.

I turned real quick to see Clyde fall to the floor, blood spurting out of the back of his head.

And then I saw Charlie, the gun in his hand. His eyes, like I said before, were blank like he wasn't even in there. He walked to Dracula to stand beside him. He had to step right over Clyde's body to do it and he didn't once even look down.

"Charlie!" I screamed. "Don't do this!"

I knew what was happening. Charlie had eaten Dracula's blood off the journal pages. Charlie belonged to Dracula. He had all along, ever since he'd first eaten the blood. Maybe he'd known this at some level, but I don't think so. My guess is he feared it might be that way, but had no way of knowing for sure.

"Your brother is mine," said Dracula. "Forever onward. I suppose it could have been different, but then again, perhaps not." Dracula's expression wasn't one of gloating, maybe more of sorrow. I can't really say. All I know is there I was facing Dracula with my brother standing right next to him ready to put a bullet in me if I made a move.

Mavis was still screaming and grabbing for the knife in her neck.

Dracula stroked Charlie's hair like he was a dog or something. And then he bit into his neck. All the while, Charlie kept the gun aimed at me. Dracula was clamped to his neck, sucking his life away, and he just stood there ready to shoot his own brother.

It was then that Pearl came back into the room. I'd only barely wondered where she was. Things were so crazy and moving so fast. She had three bottles of schnapps in her hands. Each had a rag sticking out of it. The rags were lit on fire.

She paused for a moment, at the sight of her dead uncle. I thought she might fall into hysterics or run to his corpse, but this look of hatred landed on her face and she hurled one of the bottles at Dracula with this horrible screeching cry. It hit him on the right arm, shattering. The schnapps burst into flames.

Dracula was on fire. Pearl threw the next one at Mavis. It hit her on the back and, whoosh! Flames all over. Screaming and hooting, she stumbled toward the window and tumbled out through the shattered glass.

Dracula was distracted so I grabbed Charlie real quick, knocked the gun from his hand and pulled him away from the flaming vampire. He was dazed, looking back at Dracula like a lost puppy, but letting me guide him toward the door.

Dracula screamed and howled curses in what I'm guessing was his native language.

Pearl threw the last bottle and I have to say the girl has aim because she hit Dracula square in the face.

He was like a bonfire now, screeching in this high-pitched wail.

The flames were spreading though. Some of the furniture had already caught due to the splashing and the rug and wood floor was on fire.

"Hurry! Grab Ma," I screamed to Pearl as I pulled Charlie toward the doorway. He stumbled along with me, his eyes still blank, two big gashes in his neck. I got him outside onto the front lawn and then rushed back inside to help Pearl with Ma.

We pulled her outside and nearly down to the street. By this point the curtains had caught fire and then one of the walls. I could tell already, the whole place was going up.

Ma was dead, but I kept trying to wake her, slapping her face, pounding on her chest, pressing my hands against her bloody neck. She couldn't be gone. She just couldn't.

I guess I was in my own world, because all of a sudden I realized Pearl was pulling on my arm.

"Johnny! Johnny! Where's Mavis? We don't know if she's still out here?"

And then it struck me. "Forget Mavis. Where's Charlie?"

And I looked up just in time to see him stepping back into the burning house. I ran after him. But the flames were too hot. I couldn't get through the door. I tried. I really tried. But I couldn't even see anything through the flames. It was just like Charlie evaporated into the inferno. The roof was buckling, the whole place groaning like a demon. And just like that, he was gone. Charlie was gone.

It's been four nights now. The house burned to the ground. There was no sign of remains for either Dracula or Charlie. Clyde's body was found and so was Earl's. I'd like to decapitate Earl's body, but it's still at the coroner. He's probably truly dead though. He'd had a knife through the heart and then was burned to a crisp.

We never did find Mavis.

Charlie's journal and Uncle Abraham's chest was at Clyde's house because he was reading through the stuff looking for clues. I guess that's a good thing the stuff was saved, but at this point I don't really care.

Pearl and me had to tell a pretty tall tale to the police. Clyde had a bullet in his head after all, and Earl had a knife in the chest. But we blamed Capone. Well, not him exactly. I sure don't want him coming after us again. But on bootleggers in general. I told the cops we were out of the business but still had some of our stock in the place. So a bunch a thugs raided us for our liquor.

I guess they bought it.

I don't really care.

I lost my brother and my ma that night, Pearl lost her uncle, and I still don't know if we really killed Dracula or not. I don't really care much about anything else.

From the journal of Charles Van Helsing
September 12, 1939

I followed Johnny again tonight. He'd gone to the market to get groceries for the family. Pearl and the children were at home and he was alone as he made his way down the narrow street. Johnny sensed me as he often does. He paused, turned, searched the darkness, his eyes narrow, his posture cautious. He never sees me. At least, I don't think he's ever seen me. But he knows. I'm certain that he knows.

As always, I struggled with the temptation to bring him into the eternal midnight. Oh, I know it would be wrong, such an evil thing to do to one's own brother, but, well, to be together again, to be able to share with him the misery and the glory of a potentially eternal existence. Would that be so bad, really? Well, not tonight. For whatever reason, I can never quite bring myself to do it. Not tonight. But someday. Yes, someday.

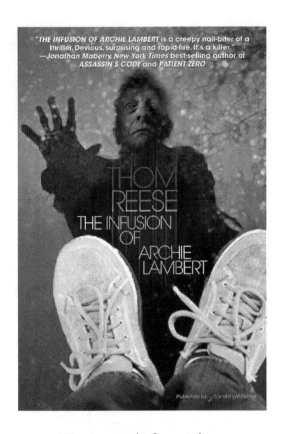

For more information
visit:

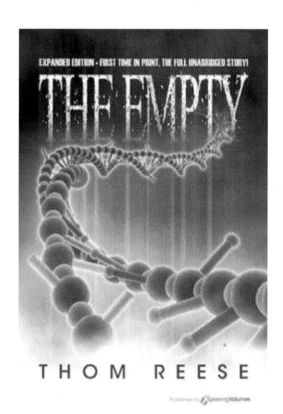

EXPANDED EDITION - FIRST TIME IN PRINT, THE FULL UNABRIDGED STORY!

THE EMPTY

THOM REESE

For more information
visit: www.speakingvolumes.us

For more information
visit: www.speakingvolumes.us

For more information
visit: www.speakingvolumes.us

Sign up for free and bargain books

Join the Speaking Volumes mailing list

Text

ILOVEBOOKS

to 22828 to get started.

Message and data rates may apply.

Made in the USA
Las Vegas, NV
28 November 2023

81698904R00083